### *"Casey Cavanaugh is rodeo!"*

The girl gave a hollow little laugh. "He's been bull-riding champ and bareback champ and he's the current all-around champ. He's who the fans are interested in. He's who all the news people are interested in."

"But I thought you said he didn't give interviews," Paige said.

"He doesn't," the girl replied. "But you wanted to know who was interesting, who you should talk to. He's who. And," she added with a trace of bitterness, "the way he's been looking at you, who knows? He might even give you an interview. You'd be famous overnight."

Dear Reader:

Romance offers us all so much. It makes us "walk on sunshine." It gives us hope. It takes us out of our own lives, encouraging us to reach out to others. Janet Dailey is fond of saying that romance is a state of mind, that it could happen anywhere. Yet nowhere does romance seem to be as good as when it happens *here*.

Starting in February 1986, Silhouette Special Edition will feature the AMERICAN TRIBUTE—a tribute to America, where romance has never been so wonderful. For six consecutive months, one out of every six Special Editions will be an episode in the AMERICAN TRIBUTE, a portrait of the lives of six women, all from Oklahoma. Look for the first book, *Love's Haunting Refrain* by Ada Steward, as well as stories by other favorites—Jeanne Stephens, Gena Dalton, Elaine Camp and Renee Roszel. You'll know the AMERICAN TRIBUTE by its patriotic stripe under the Silhouette Special Edition border.

AMERICAN TRIBUTE—six women, six stories, starting in February.

AMERICAN TRIBUTE—one of the reasons Silhouette Special Edition is just that—Special.

The Editors at Silhouette Books

# CAITLIN CROSS
# High Risk

*Silhouette Special Edition*

Published by Silhouette Books New York

**America's Publisher of Contemporary Romance**

SILHOUETTE BOOKS
300 E. 42nd St., New York, N.Y. 10017

ISBN: 0-373-09272-5

First Silhouette Books printing November 1985

10 9 8 7 6 5 4 3 2 1

America's Publisher of Contemporary Romance

Printed in the U.S.A.

## CAITLIN CROSS

started writing a long time ago. Not that she's so old, but she's done a lot of living. For the first seven years of married life she traveled the rodeo circuit with her husband, who is a champion rodeo rider. When their first child was born, they decided to settle down on a farm near Norman, Oklahoma, where she attended the University of Oklahoma and graduated after concentrating on creative writing. Their family gradually expanded to include two more children. For the past three years, Caitlin has managed a clothing store specializing in Western wear and sportswear, but she has recently abandoned the retail world and has a new career as a romance writer.

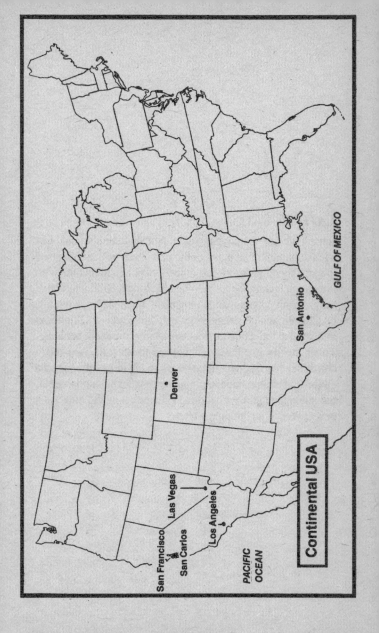

## Chapter One

It was the same. Colder maybe, but otherwise the same. Denver airport varied little from San Francisco airport. The same concrete and traffic and crowds. No soaring eagles. No fur-decked mountain men. Just as she had expected.

She waited beside the curb, her matched luggage at her feet, every hair in place, the skirt of her carefully chosen, wool traveling suit neatly smoothed. She felt no disappointment. In spite of Trisha's excitement, she hadn't really believed Denver would be any different. The girl had been so sure that the mile-high city was a grand and magical place. Paige saw the difference in their expectations as simple. Trish was a twelve-year-old who was still full of dreams, while she herself was a twenty-six-year-old who had been steeped in reality.

An unmarked beige van braked to a halt in front of her. The driver was a girl in blue jeans and parka who looked more suited to leading cheers at Denver U than to ferrying passengers.

"Stouffer's Inn shuttle!" the girl called loudly, and a stampede of people shoved past Paige to board.

She held back, watching, distancing herself from the laughing, chattering crowd good-naturedly packing themselves into the vehicle. No, Denver was not any different. She had the same sense of apartness. The same feeling of not fitting in or belonging. Like the only piece saved from a puzzle that had long since been discarded.

"Would this seat be all right ma'am?" the girl driver asked deferentially, indicating the single front-passenger position.

"Yes, thank you," Paige said, rousing herself from her thoughts and maneuvering as gracefully as possible into the high seat. She perched stiffly, acutely self-conscious of her conspicuous position in the van full of people.

There were so many simultaneous conversations being conducted that they formed a solid wave of sound drifting toward her. Individual words or parts of sentences were indistinguishable. She watched as the hand that should have held a pompon ground the gears into reverse.

The girl scanned the rearview mirror while blowing and popping a series of small pink bubbles. "Next stop Stouffer's Inn," she announced loudly to the back of the van, and then turned to Paige. "Sometimes we get people on the wrong shuttle if I don't do

all that yelling," the girl confided. "Get's pretty confusing for folks during rodeo week. The hotel's so
busy it has to hire these extra vans, and they aren't
painted with the name or anything. Plus they hire
lots of temporary help—like me," she said with a
grin, "and none of us have uniforms."

Several large bubbles appeared and disappeared as
the van inched along in traffic. Paige stared out the
front window at the small melting patches of gray
snow beside the road. She had only seen snow on
film. It had always looked so beautiful.

"You here on business?" the girl asked.

"Yes," Paige answered.

"I figured you were. You shoulda saved it till after
the rodeo and stock show, though. It'll be pretty wild
and crazy and crowded around here this week." The
girl chuckled out loud. "Just talkin' about it gives me
chills. I can hardly wait! The real cowboys are startin'
to come in. I mean the *real* ones! And they always
stay here. You talk about parties.... That's the reason
I get this job every year. Have to cut my classes, but
it's worth it!" She stopped and glanced at Paige as
though suddenly feeling guilty. "It'll probably be a
real hassle for you, though, trying to avoid it all."

"I won't be trying to avoid it. I'm here because of
the rodeo," Paige said, hoping that would put an end
to the conversation.

"You're kidding!" the girl exclaimed. "You?"

"Yes," Paige said, irritated at the girl's probing.
"Don't women come to Denver during rodeo week?"

"Sure," the girl answered quickly. "Tons of women.
All kinds. All ages. Lots of la-de-da types, you know,

playboy bunnies and stuff.'' She shrugged as if resigned to inescapable facts. 'Everybody's after a cowboy. A *real* cowboy... but I never figured you for that.''

Paige had to smile. The idea that she had come to Colorado ''after a cowboy'' was amusingly absurd. ''I'm here on business,'' she said simply. ''Strictly business.''

''Good.'' The girl sounded relieved. ''I couldn't imagine you getting anywhere... with cowboys, I mean. Not that you're not pretty and all.'' Her voice took on a note of distress. ''You're just not the type.... You know. The fun-and-party type. The type cowboys go for.'' She blushed a deep crimson. ''Don't get me wrong... I don't mean any of this as a putdown. I really admire ladies like you. In fact, someday when I'm finished having my fun and I get older, I hope I can be just as classy and sophisticated as you are.''

The girl seemed to realize suddenly that she was only inserting her foot more firmly in her mouth. Still red-cheeked, she simply stopped talking and pointedly turned her full attention to the road.

Paige studied the padded dashboard. What was bothering her? Certainly not the idea that a girl of nineteen or twenty thought her ''older.'' She remembered how ancient twenty-six had sounded when she was only nineteen.

She turned to look out the side window and there she was, Paige Ann Bannister, framed in the silvered square of the wide-angle mirror. Hair fastened firmly in the usual topknot. Minimum of makeup. Minimum of jewelry. Definitely not the party type. Never had been. Never would be. Except for Christmas at the office, the last party she remembered attending had been for eighth-grade graduation. Simple facts. So what was bothering her?

Maybe it was the dawning realization, after all these years, that she had missed a vital part of life. A part of growing up. That the carefree times, the fun and party and boy-crazy times had a definite place in the journey to maturity. And now that the journey was over for her, she could look back and see what had been irretrievably lost during those years when she had been both surrogate mother to her sisters and nurse to her invalid mother.

Now that she was an adult woman and firmly ensconced in respectability. Now that her mother was gone and her father had remarried and her sisters were tucked away in college. Now that the struggles were over. Now she could look back and feel a loss. This giddy young girl beside her illustrated more poignantly than ever that wonderful stage of life she had missed. That gay, passionately carefree stage of life that, once passed, she knew could never be recaptured.

She stared out at the dirty snow and the profusion of airliners. How could eagles be expected to soar when there were 747s in the flight path.

She wished she were back in San Francisco, sitting at her desk. She longed for the familiarity of the office. The faces, the furniture, the known quantities. She wanted to sit down at her drawing board and see all the pens and pencils and assorted tools arranged in tidy little compartments. At work she fit in. There was a place for her. She belonged.

The sudden jarring stop in front of the hotel cut off Paige's thoughts. She stepped out into the broad, porticoed entryway and stood. People streamed by her. She was in no hurry. The luggage from the van—including her matched set—was trundled inside. The massive wooden doors opened and shut, opened and shut. She reached up to smooth nonexistent stray wisps of hair and straightened her perfect traveling suit.

Apprehension clutched at her like a giant hand. What was she doing here? She didn't belong at this hotel. She didn't belong in this town. She knew absolutely nothing about rodeo. And she had no business being on this assignment at all.

John Casey Cavanaugh watched the colorful, swirling scene before him intently. He was and always had been an avid observer of human nature. He enjoyed any gathering more when he could stand apart and watch, and he particularly relished times like the present when, due to his grubby, unsuitable appearance, he was able to observe without being recognized or approached.

There were people everywhere. They were standing in groups, gathered on the couches flanking the fireplace, clustered in chairs against the walls and waiting in lines at the long front desk. The person he was waiting for, a bellman, was nowhere to be seen.

The big front doors opened again. More people. More women. Short women. Tall women. Women in minks and ski parkas. Women in pants and dresses. Women with ready laughter and wandering eyes. His world was full of women. Still, she caught his eye.

He watched her cross the room and take her place in the registration line. Her walk was unhurried, graceful, yet full of purpose. Her skirt was modestly cut, but that did not keep him from visualizing the entire length of her slender legs as she moved. Her dark, coppery hair was done up, but he could tell it was thick and long. She turned to glance about the room, and he saw that her face was a perfect classic oval.

Her dark woolen suit was all wrong, he decided. She should have on a long dress and little gloves and be holding a sun parasol. A well-bred young lady from out of a Victorian painting.

She seemed to be alone. Maybe she was unattached. Not that being attached seemed to make any difference to anyone these days. Lots of women came to his bed with their wedding rings on. She looked different though. Like a lady. A real lady. If there was still such a thing.

He wanted to meet her. The realization came as a surprise to him. He spent most of his energies trying to avoid the constantly changing, nameless women who crowded into his life.

The line moved up and she was swallowed by a wall of people. It was the check-in line. She was staying. He might have a chance. Although he wasn't certain how to go about meeting someone like her. She probably didn't talk to strangers, much less accept invitations for dinner. And if she would talk to him he wasn't sure he'd know what to say. Women had been chasing him for so long he'd forgotten all the polite conversational niceties of the dating ritual. There had to be a way, though. Every problem had a solution.

He turned his attention back to the matter at hand. The bell captain was supposed to be holding an important package for him. So far all the bellmen had been so busy delivering luggage that he hadn't been able to nail any of them for even a moment. He was getting impatient.

It had been a long trip. Nothing had gone right. He had started out in his own plane, a Beachcraft Bonanza. Being a fully qualified, instrument-rated pilot, he was capable of handling a myriad of minor difficulties that could and often did crop up in a flight. Fortunately for his busy schedule, major problems seldom occurred. Major problems spelled ground time.

When the oil had begun seeping out of the engine cowling and spattering on the windscreen in midflight that was major. Ground-time major.

He had landed immediately and tried to arrange repairs. The parts hadn't been available. He had checked with all the airlines for an open seat to Denver. They'd been booked solid for days. There'd been no rental cars available. He had finally talked the airport's elderly janitor into parting with his own vehicle, a wheezy little economy car, for an outrageous amount. The car wouldn't do over forty-five, and it had taken him all night and half the day to make it in.

His eyes felt like sandpaper and his jaw was covered with stubble. His dark hair felt full of grit and oil from his plane's engine, and there was oil and grease on his jeans, as well. He badly needed to clean up and maybe even grab a few hours of sleep if he was going to be in any shape for that press party tonight.

Still no available bellman. He was tired and his patience was at an end. He'd waited long enough. Finding a package couldn't be that difficult. He moved around to the back of the wooden stand and ducked behind it to sort through the mounds of envelopes and boxes.

Paige walked across the crowded lobby with the room key gripped tightly in her hand. She hadn't known the reservation would be under Trends, Unlimited, instead of Bannister. The resulting confusion had turned the simple registration process into an ordeal.

Then there was the luggage situation. When she had requested that her bags be sent up immediately, the clerk had politely detailed the plight of the harried bellmen. Due to the rodeo, hundreds of guests were all checking in at once. In spite of all the temporary help added in that department, it was physically impossible to deliver everyone's luggage immediately upon check-in. He followed the explanation with a sincere apology.

Inwardly on the verge of panic, Paige had patiently explained about the press party that evening. And about her role in it. And about the necessity of getting her notes—which she had foolishly packed in a suitcase—and belongings to her room as soon as possible. The man was sympathetic but doubtful when he suggested that she go to the bell captain's stand. There she might find a bellman on duty with whom she could try to make special arrangements.

Paige strode purposefully across the lobby toward the captain's stand. She resolved not to let either the external irritations or the inner uncertainties destroy her control. She would handle this, as she did everything, in a calm but firm manner.

Mounds of suitcases, skis, boxes and all nature of possessions filled the area designated for luggage. The focus was the captain's stand, taller than a speaker's podium and as wide as a desk. Several people lounged around the perimeter, but there was no one in sight who looked like a bellman, either temporary or permanent.

Drawing closer to the stand, Paige realized with relief that there was indeed a man working behind it. He was bending over, sorting through some things, and had been previously out of her line of vision. She caught a glimpse of his gray sweatshirt and grease-stained jeans. He was obviously another temporary.

"Excuse me," she said, "I have a problem with my bags...."

The man straightened as though startled and turned toward her in one fluid motion. Suddenly she was looking into dark-blue eyes, deep dark-blue eyes, and she was totally, and inexplicably, flustered.

"I...ah...tonight I have a...well, my luggage is..." She gestured vaguely as she tried to explain.

She finally stopped her verbal fumbling and cleared her throat softly as if to imply that the problem with her speech was entirely physical. She couldn't remember ever having felt this awkward.

She was completely unaware of the commotion behind her. Unaware of the soft swinging arc of the duffel bag until it connected with her legs and unceremoniously knocked her off her feet. She sat there on the floor, robbed of all dignity and dazed from more than the fall, amid a flurry of exclamations and apologies from the owner of the bag and assorted bystanders.

Casey was amazed at his good fortune. Here she was, his Victorian painting, and she had actually spoken to him. He had no idea what she had been talking about, but that wasn't important. What was important was that she was here, sitting on the floor, and he had an incomparable chance to introduce himself.

He bent over her, searching her face for a sign of pain, hoping she wasn't actually hurt. To his relief her clear green eyes held only embarrassment.

Her skirt was midthigh, and he had to tear his gaze from the lace-edged corner of her slip and the exposed length of stockinged leg. He reached out instinctively to help her up, and then grew suddenly uncertain. His arms felt disturbingly personal around her. He jerked them free as though he'd been suddenly warned not to touch.

She looked up at him quizzically, then held out her hands for assistance. He was riveted by the sight of them. There was not a ring to be seen, and there was no telltale white circle on that important left finger. He took hold of them gently. They were soft and warm and so small in his.

She started to rise, her creeping skirt tantalizing him further, and he misjudged his strength in his efforts to help her gain her feet. He yanked her up and directly into his body. He felt the soft crush of her breasts and breathed the whispery clean scent of her hair before she quickly pulled back.

She seemed so confused, so shaken, that he wanted to reassure her in some way. He moved back around the stand, putting a solid oak barrier between them in an effort to make her feel secure.

She took a deep breath. Her blouse was high-collared and buttoned to the top. Her suit jacket hung open. Even with all that cloth he couldn't help but notice the swell of her breasts as she drew the air into her lungs.

He was almost ashamed. This was a lady, not another groupie on the make. The least he could do was keep his eyes and thoughts under control.

"What I was trying to say," she began hesitantly, "is that I need to ask a favor of you."

He couldn't believe it. He simply couldn't believe it!

"Do you know who I am, then?" he asked in wonder.

"Of course. I mean, I couldn't tell by the way you're dressed, but the desk clerk told me I might find you here."

He was dumbstruck. All he could do was stare. He wished suddenly that he looked more presentable. "You were looking for me?" he asked in puzzled disbelief.

"Yes." She smiled with a genuine warmth that was

reflected in her clear eyes. "I may be the first, but if you stay here long enough there will probably be hordes of others after you for the same reason."

He watched with fascination as she produced a large brass room key. He still hadn't the foggiest idea what she wanted.

"I know this is a little irregular," she said as she placed the key on the wooden surface between them, "but I have a very important function tonight, and time is slipping away—and...well, I would really appreciate it if you could fit me in."

She couldn't have meant what he thought she meant.

"What?" he said, feeling as stupid as he sounded.

"I know how busy you are," she said, her voice close to pleading. "And I know I'm lucky even to have caught you, but considering the circumstances and the fact that there seems to be no one else available, I really am in need of your services."

Casey's entire fantasy shattered into tiny fragments. She wanted him to come to her room! Services! That was a new one. And a time limit, no less. He'd never had a woman come right out and ask for a quickie. And that business about him being the only one available right now. Huh! Usually they weren't so obvious about the fact that any one of the big names would do.

She was nothing but another groupie. Classy-looking, maybe, but nothing more than a common buckle polisher making her play. His life was full of women, but there were no ladies. There was no one he could respect or trust. His disappointment was so keen it was actually physical.

He turned his back to her and knelt down to give his attention back to the package hunt.

"Try me another time," he said, attempting to keep his voice light, but the cynicism was there nonetheless. "Right now I'm too tired."

She moved around to stand in front of him. "Please, I realize how exhausting this all must be for you, but it's very, very important to me. Please."

He'd never had such a "ladylike" proposition before. It was almost funny. The chick had quite a little act. He wondered how far she carried it in the bedroom.

He looked up at the classic face, and then let his gaze travel freely down her slender body and up again. She wasn't what he'd imagined. What he wanted. She was no better than all the others, but he had to admit he still found the package, and the act, damn attractive. She would be good for a few days' fun. Maybe even the run of the rodeo. She'd made it clear that she'd take whoever was available. If he didn't grab his chance now she'd probably hook up with one of the other guys before the afternoon was over.

"Sure," he said finally. "What the hell."

Paige didn't understand this man before her, one minute so open, dark eyes full of warmth, and the next minute cynical and cold. But, then, that was why she avoided most men. She didn't ever understand them. Starting with her father.

The father who had usually come home smelling of whiskey and cheap perfume hours after his night job had let off. The father who had never been satisfied regardless of how hard her mother worked and scrimped and who, after her mother's stroke, had never recognized Paige's efforts. The same father who called her "Annie" and had brought her a puppy on her tenth birthday. The same father who had wept for days after her mother's death. No, she had never been able to understand any man.

She based her judgments of men on pure instinct. It seldom failed her. Her snap judgments were usually sound. Sometimes she thought of them as her survival instincts. They were all that kept her safe in the world of dating and men. And her instincts were strong right now. This man was trouble. Big trouble.

Paige willed her cheeks not to turn pink when he so pointedly looked her up and down. Anger or embarrassment would not help matters. She was determined to remain calm and in control.

Suddenly the man scooped up her key and started across the floor as though leaving.

"Wait," she called in confusion, "my luggage...." She gestured toward the piles of belongings. "I need my luggage."

He shot her an irritated look. "You mean you don't have *any* of your things yet?" he demanded.

"Of course not," she said. "When would I have gotten them?" She took a breath and consciously eliminated the harsh edge that had begun to creep into her voice. "Listen, I'll help you find it and we'll make fast work of this, I promise."

Was the man a simpleton? Maybe that explained why he was so down on his luck. Why he'd had to resort to low-paying temporary employment and why he had such a disheveled appearance. She considered the theory a moment and then discarded it. No, he was no dummy. There was something about him that belied stupidity. Something in his manner that promised intelligence and self-assurance.

She ferreted out her luggage and watched as he retrieved each piece from its hiding place. Maybe this was just a part-time job for him. He was above standard college age, but he could still be a student. Or maybe he worked mornings as a mechanic or something and didn't have time to clean up between shifts. Maybe he was just a hard-working man holding down two jobs to support a wife and children. Wife. The thought was strangely disappointing.

Paige shook herself mentally. She didn't even know this man. He was a total stranger. It was no concern of hers whether he was married or single, or whether he might have to hold down twenty jobs to support his family. She did decide to tip generously, though, just in case.

She picked up her carryon and watched as he hoisted the rest of the load and started out across the floor. Not exactly like the movies, she thought, but at least he was getting the job done. She followed him across the crowded lobby. He moved easily, his broad shoulders and muscular arms effortlessly supporting her heavy cases.

He didn't have on a wedding ring, she noted. But, then, that meant little where men were concerned. Most of the married men in her office never wore their rings.

Casey set down the bags, unlocked the door and watched her walk inside ahead of him. How could she look and act so wonderful and be just another camp follower? Women never failed to mystify him.

He shut the door, placed all the cases in the open closet and turned to watch her. She was absorbed in searching through her purse for something. He crossed the floor and shut the heavy draperies. The room was cast in shadow.

She dropped her purse and turned to fumble with a lamp. He moved up quickly behind her, caught her wrist and turned her around to face him. He could hear her breathing pick up in the stillness.

"Are you interested in any chitchat," he asked.

"No," she answered quickly, and backed up a few steps. "Now I want to thank you for..."

He continued moving toward her and she continued retreating, until her back was against the wall. She wasn't nearly as aggressive as he'd thought she would be. He leaned in close, resting his hands on the wall on either side of her head. He could smell her hair again. It reminded him of wildflowers. He kissed her lightly, barely brushing her lips with his.

"Please," she said in a trembling, childlike voice, and pushed against his chest with her hands.

He accepted this as a request for more, and pressed his body against hers as he kissed her long and hard. He could feel his body awakening. He could feel... *pain!* Hard sharp pain. She'd bitten him!

He pulled back in surprise, and she landed a healthy slap on his cheek.

"Get out!" she ordered, and pointed toward the door. "Out!"

He backed toward the door, leery of another attack. The woman was obviously crazy.

"I ought to report you," she threatened. "Is that the way you collect all your tips?"

She followed him as he made his escape into the hallway and then tossed a crumpled bill onto the carpet at his feet.

"I was going to give you more, but you don't deserve it. You don't deserve to work at a reputable hotel—as a bellman or anything else!" she threw at him as she slammed the door.

The full meaning of her angry torrent didn't sink in until after the door had stopped vibrating from the force of its closing.

Bellman? What had she meant? He looked down at his clothes. Could it be... had she thought... Of course! He'd been behind that captain's stand, and she'd thought he was one of the temporary help. How could he have been so stupid! All she'd wanted was her luggage. And he had come on like some kind of animal! Had he lost touch with the outside world? Had he become so programmed by his life-style that he was blind to innocent motives?

Suddenly his spirits rose. He'd been wrong! She was a lady, after all. A real lady. Everything he'd imagined. He looked at the closed door before him and his heart sank. She'd probably never speak to him again. It was going to take a lot of work to smooth out this mistake.

Paige fumbled the locks into place and leaned heavily against the door. Her whole body was shaking.

When he had first kissed her, so soft and light, she should have kicked his shins. But she'd enjoyed it. She was almost ashamed to admit it to herself. The kiss had been a recreation of her youthful fantasies. Then he had pressed closer and his lips had been demanding, and it wasn't fantasy anymore. It was a terribly frightening reality.

Had she done something to lead him on? She thought not. He must just assume that all single women were hungry for his attentions. No wonder he liked being a bellman. She could imagine how many lonely women travelers there must be. Her instincts had been right again. There was some comfort in that.

She straightened and drew in a cleansing breath.

Hopefully she would never see him again, never sense those dark eyes studying her. To think she had actually felt something toward him—some strange emotional response—in spite of the inner warnings she had heard. It was all just further proof of something she already knew: her instincts were usually sound and it was foolish as well as dangerous to go against them.

She clicked on a light and moved to survey her temporary home. It was pleasant and comfortable. Thick chocolate carpeting, tasteful prints on linen-toned walls, walnut furniture. She adjusted the heavy rust drapes so she could look out at the sharp, clear blueness of the January sky.

Settled now, she dug the notes out of her big suitcase and sat down to read.

**PRESS PARTY for RODEO CHAMPIONS STOUFFER'S INN 8:00 P.M.**

The words were underlined in red. She knew that part of her schedule already. She wished that when her boss had handed the thick packet to her at the airport she hadn't been so nervous. Maybe then she would have realized that zipping the papers into her suitcase meant she wouldn't be able to read them on the plane.

It was still hard for her to believe that she was here and expected to carry out this assignment. She, who only wrote brief lines of copy to fit neatly into ads, or minor press releases that required only a phone call for research. She was supposed to step in with no preparation, no prior knowledge of rodeo and replace a top-notch veteran who had fallen ill. Maggie Carson, her boss, had lost her mind!

When she had studied the material to the point of memorization she let her head fall back against the chair and closed her eyes. Weariness washed over her. She checked her watch, calculated that there was indeed time for a short nap and then pulled the drapes closed.

She woke sometime later from a troubled, dream-ridden sleep full of a man with dark-blue eyes who both frightened and intrigued her. The disturbing images clouded her mind until her work-related worries reared their heads and crowded all other thoughts out.

Through the process of getting ready she asked herself—why had Miss Carson manipulated her into this assignment? She had never requested fieldwork. She was perfectly happy with her position as a staff writer for the public relations firm of Trends, Unlimited. She had never aspired to any higher status.

She reached up to feel the thick figure eight of hair at the nape of her neck. It was fastened securely. She slipped the tiny gold studs, a long-ago present from her mother, into her ears. It was time. She glanced in the mirror at the hemline of her beige wool dress. No slip showing. Then she gathered up her tiny tape recorder and her key and tucked them into her purse.

There was only one consolation to this evening, she thought as she headed out the door. That horrible bellman could not possibly be working at such a select function as this.

She headed down the wide, carpeted corridor and found herself wishing she had been able to contact Judy Williams. Judy Reynolds now, of course. The woman had been a friend in grammar school and part of high school. Until the Williams family moved away to Utah. Now the relationship was down to Christmas cards, but still Paige had no doubt that Judy would help her. Theirs had been that kind of friendship. And if anyone would know the ins and outs of professional rodeo it would be Judy. She had married a pro cowboy, a bull rider.

The assignment had been so sudden and the trip arrangements so rushed that Paige had had only one chance to call Judy. Paige's heart had sunk when a baby-sitter answered and said Mr. and Mrs. Reynolds were gone for more than a week. The bright spot came when the sitter went on to add that the couple was en route to Denver and could be contacted the following day at Stouffer's Inn.

If she could only get by until she had a chance to learn more from Judy.

Paige's steps slowed as she neared her destination. Finally she came to a complete halt. She stood there in the center of the hallway about thirty feet from the door and watched the activity. A large, stern-faced man in hotel uniform was checking for invitations and passes. The people entering were in a gay mood, but he never smiled as he admitted them. It was as if he were stationed there to remind her that this was a serious business. A very serious business.

Despair settled heavily on her shoulders and clutched frantically at her stomach. How in the world could she handle this? Was it the end? The end of her long sought-after job at Trends? The end of her career ambitions, modest though they were? Would she be demoted, humiliated, possibly even fired?

Maggie Carson's kind, patient face filled her mind. Maggie believed she could do this. Paige had to try. She had to jump in and give it her best.

She drew in a deep breath, squared her shoulders and marched straight up to the entrance. The serious doorman took a quick look at her invitation and waved her inside.

Casey saw her come in. He'd known she would, and he'd been waiting. Armed with just her room number, he had managed to find out her name and the purpose of her visit to Denver. He had stationed himself in a perfect position to scan arrivals, yet remain unnoticed among the crowd himself.

He watched her enter the room tentatively and stand near the wall. Her lustrous hair was fastened low on her head this time. He wondered how long it was. Would it fall all the way to her waist? That incredibly small waist beneath the crushed leather belt?

She looked so good. So poised and cool and wonderful. He wanted to rush right up to her and try to explain the afternoon's mix-up. But he knew that wouldn't work. He had to bide his time, wait for the right opportunity. Meanwhile it was a pleasure just to watch her.

## Chapter Two

Paige stepped into the room, and was engulfed by a kaleidoscope of color and noise. Waves of excitement hit her with a physical impact.

She inched her way along the wall, so lost in the moment that she forgot her fears. She had no notion of where or how to begin. She felt like a swimmer on the edge of a huge, glittering pool, unable to decide whether to wade in slowly or plunge in headfirst.

The decision was taken out of her hands when two of the most rugged-looking men she had ever seen descended on her.

"Say there, lil' lady, you look downright lonely over here." He was a big, cocky man of about thirty, and as he spoke he threw a beefy arm around Paige's shoulders.

Her initial reaction was to give him the customary brush-off and cold shoulder she used with all men who came on to her. Then she realized that this might be just the break she needed. She shrugged his arm off in as polite a manner as she could muster, smiled and said, "I'm so glad I found you two gentlemen. I was looking for some very special material on rodeo, and you two are perfect."

The two men beamed at each other and then at her.

"Do either of you have wives here?" she asked. "If you do I'd like to include them."

"Huh," the big man snorted, "you won't find many wives in this business."

"Oh. Well, do you mind if I tape?" she asked, readying her cassette.

Both men shrugged and grinned and did a "yeah, sure, okay" routine so she took a deep breath and pushed the record button.

"World Championship Press Party, tape one," she announced to the machine, trying to mimic a veteran newsman she had watched only moments ago. It had sounded so impressive when he'd done it.

"Now would each of you please state your name and event."

The interview was no sizzler, but in spite of her lack of knowledge she did come out with some solid material. The cocky man turned out to be the new World Champion Steer Wrestler and the younger, shyer one was the Rookie of the Year in that event. She thought it a pretty respectable effort for her first day, and some of the stories about the horses they used for competition were actually verging on terrific.

She thanked both the men, and immediately the huge arm encircled her shoulders again.

"Hey, how 'bout when this thing's over we could get together and I could give ya some really good stories," the man suggested.

Again she shrugged off the arm. "I couldn't possibly take up any more of your time," she said with a professional smile. "And now if you will excuse me, I must get back to work."

Paige made her escape and headed straight for the nearest, most likely looking subject she could spot. Quickly she introduced herself and explained her purpose. She'd guessed correctly. The petite young woman in the wine-colored hat was someone interesting. She turned out to be the Rookie of the Year in the Women's Barrel Racing.

Paige was immersed in a meaty discussion with the girl, getting some fascinating insights into how it felt to be competing in the only women's events in professional rodeo, when a commotion occurred across the room. Both she and the barrel racer automatically turned their attention toward it. Several people around them rushed forward eagerly. Clearly something of interest was happening. Paige made an effort to see the source, but the knot of people completely obscured whoever or whatever was causing the stir.

"It's just Casey," the girl said, as though that explained everything.

"Who?" Paige asked quickly.

"Casey Cavanaugh," the girl said, and looked at Paige strangely. "He's got this thing about not giving interviews, and every once in a while, when a reporter really keeps after him, he'll get to kind of arguing—in a funny sort of way—about why he won't do the interview. Everybody who knows him loves to watch the show."

"How did you know that's what was going on?" Paige asked.

"I've been watching him," the girl admitted. "It's a bad habit of mine."

"Watching people?"

"No, watching Casey."

She looked almost sad for a moment, and then, eyeing Paige carefully, she said, "He's been watching you all evening."

Paige was taken completely by surprise.

"I can't imagine why," she said finally.

The barrel racer stared off into the crowd. Her discomfort was evident. The mood of the interview was gone, and Paige knew better than to continue. She wound it up quickly and thanked the woman for her time.

"You've been so helpful," Paige said, "and it's obvious you know everyone. I was wondering if you could give me any suggestions, possibly point out an interesting rodeo personality you think I should talk to."

"Casey," the girl said, giving a hollow little laugh. "He *is* rodeo. He's been bull-riding champ and bareback champ, and he's the current all-around champ. He's who the fans are interested in. He's who all the news people are interested in."

"But I thought you said he didn't give interviews," Paige said.

"He doesn't," the girl replied. "But you wanted to know who was interesting, who you should talk to. He's who. And," she added with a trace of bitterness, "the way he's been looking at you, who knows. He might even give you an interview. You'd be famous overnight."

Paige wandered through the crowd, puzzling over the girl's sudden change in attitude. It was obvious that this Casey person was occupied, so she just relaxed and let her mind go. She felt at ease in the roomful of people now. It was an open, warm group. People smiled and nodded and spoke, whether they were acquainted or not. There was no stuffiness. There were no pretensions. The rodeo people were a diverse bunch. Young and old, tall and short, well dressed or jean clad. Yet still there was a common denominator. They all radiated a special self-assurance, perhaps born of the fact that they were the tops in their field.

The gathering grew increasingly congested and noisy and Paige was ready for a break, so she retreated to the ladies' room to reload her recorder with a fresh cassette and review her progress. Things were going fine. In fact, she could even describe herself as doing quite well. She felt suddenly capable and efficient and pleased with herself.

She returned to the action with a renewed sense of self-esteem. The knot of people had broken up. Apparently the "show" was over and Mr. Cavanaugh was free again. Only she had no idea who or where he was.

She asked a likely looking man, and he gestured vaguely toward the opposite end of the room. She headed in that direction, all senses alert. She stopped again, this time asking a reporter if he knew the whereabouts of the infamous Casey. She felt herself gently taken by the shoulders, guided a few feet through the crowd and pointed directly to a man whose back was turned to her.

She thanked the reporter and stood there a moment. There was something puzzlingly familiar about the man. How could that be? She knew no one in Denver, and certainly no one in rodeo. Not counting Judy's husband, Ken, of course. And she barely knew him. After one introduction nearly five years ago she hardly recalled what Ken looked like. Maybe she had seen Casey Cavanaugh's picture somewhere. Or maybe she had seen him at the hotel. What other explanation could there be for this puzzling sense of familiarity?

She studied him closely. Even from behind she could tell he was the kind of man fantasies are made of. It was small wonder the fans and news media fawned over him. From his big black hat down to the soft leather of his gleaming, hand-worked boots the man was wonderful. His sky-blue shirt of raw silk was obviously custom-made to span the width of his broad shoulders and taper down to his lean waist. The jeans that hugged his trim hips and long legs were starched and razor creased.

Her evaluation, she assured herself, was strictly professional. Paige was not interested in meeting a man, and had she been, this one would be out of the question. If most normal, ordinary men—men who worked in offices and lived in apartments just like her—couldn't be understood or trusted, what on earth would a man who was a star athlete be like? The thought staggered her. What could she possibly say to such a man? How would she even communicate? Would he be distant and aloof, or rude and surly? Would he ignore her or insult her or politely brush her off? Or would he play the regular games? The same old "how fast can I get you into bed" games she had learned to spot in all their various forms.

She stood there, gathering her courage, when someone behind her called out a loud, "Casey!" The man she'd been focusing on turned quickly and scanned the crowd. His eyes stopped on her.

Paige was stunned.

The hair showing beneath the black hat was dark brown and wavy. The face, clean-shaven now, was outdoorsy and wonderfully tan. And the eyes—the eyes were the most incredible dark blue she'd ever seen.

Thoughts whirled crazily through her head. He couldn't be here. He was a bellman. A disheveled and disgustingly forward bellman. No, he obviously wasn't a bellman. A whole roomful of people didn't lie. He was Casey Cavanaugh. *The* Casey Cavanaugh.

So why had he been pretending to be a bellman? To win a bet? To play some kind of cruel practical joke? To seduce and then humiliate some unsuspecting woman?

She didn't care to know the answer. In fact, she didn't want to know one more thing about the infamous Casey Cavanaugh. She turned and fled.

Casey lunged into the crowd after Paige Bannister's retreating form. He had no idea what he would say to her, but he knew he had to try something. He reached out and caught hold of her elbow.

She spun around to face him the moment he touched her. Her green eyes flashed anger at him.

"Don't run off," he said lamely.

"I'm not running off," she shot back at him. "And keep your hands off me."

Quickly he held up both hands in a gesture of assent. "I'd like to talk to you," he said.

"I'm working," she answered caustically. "I don't have time for practical jokes or adolescent games."

Casey was aware of interested ears perking up all around them.

"Couldn't we just step off into a quiet corner and discuss this?" he asked.

"I can't think of anything I'd want to discuss with you," she announced haughtily.

"How about an explanation?"

She was silent, unyielding.

"How about an apology?"

She was still silent, but the very fact that she hadn't moved told him he was gaining by fractions.

"It was all a mistake. An incredibly stupid mistake. I can explain."

He looked around. A dozen pairs of eyes swiftly looked away. She was willing to listen. He had a reprieve, a chance to patch things up.

But he didn't want to go any further with the audience they'd attracted. "Right over there," he said, indicating an empty nook. "Same room. Right out in the open. Nothing to worry about. What could it hurt?"

Hesitantly she moved in just the direction he wanted her to go. He reached out instinctively to take her arm. She sent him a look of pure fire. Once again he held up his hands in a no-touch gesture and backed off a step for good measure.

He watched her moving ahead of him. Head held high. Back straight. So graceful and poised even in this crushing mass of humanity. She was so perfectly confident and in control. Yet he had seen the vulnerability in those lovely green eyes.

His gaze strayed down to the rounded curve of her hips, and he thought of placing his hands... No. He had to put those thoughts away for now. His only chance with her lay in being perfectly well behaved. The old-fashioned gentleman. He sensed that she was poised for flight and would run from him at his slightest indiscretion. He would look at and think of only her face. Nothing more.

Paige stopped when she reached the corner, turned and watched him step into place beside her. He made her feel so small and fragile—which was silly, because she judged him to be just slightly taller than herself. His nearness made her extremely uncomfortable. She backed up a step, and he had the good sense not to follow.

She looked into his eyes, but their dark intensity unnerved her, so she quickly shifted her eyes down and fastened on the dazzling gold-and-jeweled buckle at his lean waist. But that was too low, too indiscreet a direction to be looking, so she settled on the tiny CC monogrammed on his pocket flap. She could stare at that all night and feel completely secure.

A server walked by offering white wine. Casey turned and signaled for two. She was aware of the silk straining across his shoulders as he reached out. She glimpsed an expensive gold watch on his wrist, and then his strong, ringless hand was holding the stemmed glass out toward her. In slow motion she reached for it, unconscious of her movement. Her hand closed around the cold, misted glass. Her fingertips touched his. Every nerve in her body focused on that one small point of contact.

With a sharp intake of breath she pulled back as quickly as if she'd touched a hot stove. The glass dropped to the floor, splashing out the pale wine as it fell. She stared down at the puddle in dismay.

"Don't worry," he said gently. "This carpet's designed for much worse than that."

The mishap brought her back to reality. Her instincts were going wild. Caution lights flashed through her brain, and every nerve in her body tingled with alarm. "I'm still waiting for that explanation," she said firmly.

He cleared his throat and shifted his weight uneasily. "Yes. Well...to begin with I didn't realize you thought I was the bellman."

"Who was I supposed to think you were?"

"Myself. I mean...when I asked you if you knew who I was and you said yes, even though I wasn't dressed right, I thought you meant you knew I was Casey Cavanaugh, even though I looked pretty scroungy." He looked at her as though expecting a response.

"I can understand that," she said finally, and felt her stance weaken slightly.

He grinned, and she had to struggle to keep her head clear. Something didn't quite add up.

"So you didn't realize I thought you were the bellman," she said.

"I never heard you say the word 'luggage,' or maybe I would have figured it out," he explained.

"Then why did you agree to go to my room?" she asked quietly, afraid that she already knew the answer.

His grin dissolved. "It's not like it sounds. You have to understand the kind of things that go on around rodeos."

"What kind of things?" she asked.

He shrugged. "Women," he said simply.

"Women who ask you to their rooms?"

"Yes."

"And you just go—like that," she said, snapping her fingers. "Like a tomcat or a stray dog?"

"Wait a minute, you don't understand—"

"Oh, yes, I understand quite well. Not only did you behave like an animal, you put me into that category, too." She felt her body relax. There was no more need for alarm. She was back in control. The danger was over.

"Wait a minute. I didn't want you to be one of those women. I was hoping you weren't."

She hated him at that moment. Hated him for his smugness and his assumptions. Hated him for his attitudes and his casual categorizing of women. He was as bad as she'd thought he would be, maybe even worse. It was obvious that he was a user of women—and quite successful at it. But, then, how could he help but be successful, with his star status and his lean good looks and those deep, dark eyes? He had all the advantages, everything it took to make any woman easy prey.

"So you were hoping I wasn't one of 'those' women," she said in controlled anger. "You never gave me a chance to be anything else! You made an assumption, and then you set out to prove you were right. Even if I hadn't been one of 'those' women you would have tried to make me into one.

"And who are you to be labeling people, anyway? 'Those' women, indeed. Who are you to be passing judgment, as if everyone fits into either good or bad, those or nonthose?

"And even if it were a fact, if there were only two kinds of people, then the reason you are pursued by so many of 'those' women is very clearly that you are one of 'those' men!" Abruptly she turned to leave.

"Don't you at least need some rodeo information?" he asked in a bleak voice.

"No, thank you. There are dozens more people in this room to talk to, in addition to which I have a friend coming in from Utah whose husband is a bull rider. I can get information from the two of them without the experience being so unpleasant!"

Paige finished the evening's interviews in a mechanical fashion. She didn't allow herself to think until she was safely back in her room.

She felt unexplainably restless and upset. Why? The evening had gone well and her work was off to a good start. She hadn't been gone long enough to be missing Trisha. What, then? A picture of Casey Cavanaugh's arrogant face flashed through her mind, and she was suddenly overcome by anger.

Roughly she pulled the covers up around her and

bunched the pillow into a hard knot beneath her head.
The idea that a man could be so conceited as to
assume that every strange woman who spoke to him
was begging him to come to her bed! The unmiti-
gated nerve of such a man! Hot, molten anger
flowed through her, till she thought she would burst
with it. And he obviously thought she was stupid or
naive enough to buy his act, stupid enough to be his
next victim. Why else had he tried so hard with her
at the party? Damn him! Damn him for putting her
into that category.

She leaped from the bed and paced around the
room. Silently she ranted and raved about his ego-
tism, about his insulting self-serving assumption,
about his Neanderthal mind-set. Finally she collapsed
into bed from sheer exhaustion. She felt drained, and
suddenly sheepish at her loss of emotional control.
She couldn't remember ever being so angry at a man,
much less a man she barely knew. What was wrong
with her? Surely there was some unrecognized cause
to her mental turmoil.

She had always been a pragmatic person. Even during the devastation of her mother's illness and death
she had been able to sort through her emotions and
deal with them. So now she attacked her feelings and
dissected them with clinical detachment.

Was her work becoming too much for her? Was the
pressure beginning to wear her down? No, after careful analyses she was certain that her emotional state
was not related in any way to her work. Like a scien-
tist over a microscope she studied and evaluated
every aspect of her life. But she could, and had been,

dealing with it all. There was no new source of irritation or discomfort. It all came back to Casey Cavanaugh.

And if she accepted that—the fact that he was the sole cause—then she knew without a doubt that there was more. That there were feelings relating to the man, undercurrents of some sort, that she wasn't consciously aware of. Nothing else could explain her unprecedented reaction to him.

She stared sightlessly across the dark room and fought herself for more answers. Was it because he could be an important part of her assignment if only she could compromise her principles and be friendly to him? No. She truly was confident she could manage without him. Was it because she disliked making enemies in general, or maybe that she was afraid he might turn other rodeo people against her? No, that didn't seem important at all.

She pictured him. The dark blue of his eyes and the way they brightened when he looked at her—or any woman, she supposed. The tiny crescentlike furrows at the corners of his mouth when he smiled. His hands. The hard, lean strength of his body. Something stirred deep within her, and a warm current surged through her.

She was physically attracted to him! The realization hurtled through the darkness like a spear aimed at her heart.

So this was what "body chemistry" was all about. This was what she had scoffed at as a product of fiction. This was what she had come to believe could never or would never happen—at least to her. This was what she had never experienced, no matter how caring a man was or how comfortable a relationship had become.

Had he felt it, too? No, not him. Not the great Casey Cavanaugh. He was far too calloused and conceited for such a thing. She was undoubtedly just a challenge. The fish that got away.

There lay the true source of her overwhelming anger. She saw it so clearly now. She was being betrayed by nature. By her own body. She was being aroused and tempted as never before by a man who was so totally unsuitable, so completely without value or worth that it made her want to cry out with the injustice of it all.

She tossed and turned and stared out into the darkness with a fierce determination. She could handle this. She would find a way to deal with it.

She finally reasoned that she should view the entire episode as a learning experience. She had finally been struck by those legendary feelings, and now she could safely say that she very much preferred the sane, civilized approach. This was too unsettling, too frightening. She knew now, without any doubts, that she belonged in the secure, controlled life-style that called for liking a man and dating him and occasionally letting him make love to you due to a pleasantly comfortable sense of companionship and mutual interest. She imagined that if she ever did feel the need to marry, if she decided she wanted children or grew concerned about a companion for her old age, she would choose a mate using these same sensible criteria.

Her present experience proved conclusively to her the unreliability of "chemistry." Aside from physical attraction, what could she possibly find in a shallow, self-centered man like Casey Cavanaugh? Certainly nothing to base a relationship on.

She felt better, now that she had analyzed and diagnosed her malaise. She'd always believed that understanding the problem was the most important step toward solving it.

Would the physical attraction go away, now that she had recognized and acknowledged it? Probably not. Though she had used her intelligence to understand it, she doubted she could cure it by the same means. That left her with something akin to a virus during whose onslaught the patient could only rest, drink fluids and wait for time to work the magical cure.

The entire situation was frightening. For the first time in her adult life she would not be able to trust her own emotions. For the first time the difficulty would lie, not in controlling the man, but in controlling herself. Fortunately the answer to everything was blessedly simple: she would remain as far from Casey Cavanaugh as possible.

She had always been a strong person. She had every confidence she could eventually purge her thoughts of him and forget his existence.

The morning air was clear and cold outside her window, but Paige took no notice. All of her attention was focused on her reunion with Judy. The years melted away as she listened to Judy's hilarious accounts of life with Ken and her two small children.

"Now tell me all about yourself, big-time writer," Judy gently teased.

"There's not much to tell," Paige said. "At least nothing very interesting. And I'm not a big-time writer. I was the only warm body the agency had to send here. My position there is a very minor one. I do a lot of fine-print ad copy. I write some of the routine, two-paragraph releases. I was actually hired for my English skills more than my creative abilities. I'm best at proofreading and editing other people's copy. In short, my work is fairly mechanical and routine. Nothing very creative or exciting, but I like it. I'm happy there."

"So you're still belittling and underestimating yourself," Judy said.

Paige started to protest, but her friend cut her off. "Never mind. I want to hear some stories. *Something* must have happened to change you from the person I knew in high school to the classy lady you are now."

"I suppose I have changed," Paige mused, "though I can't remember being any different than I am now." Her high-school years were clouded in her mind. All of her memories seemed to center around her mother's gradually deteriorating illness. "How do you remember me?" she asked on impulse.

Judy's face grew serious. "I wouldn't tell you the complete truth," she said, "if you were still the same. But you've changed so much.... You're so beautiful and strong and...well...able to handle things, I guess. Anyway, I'm sure that the person you are now can't possibly be threatened or hurt by hearing about the entirely different person you were in high school."

Judy leaned back and her face took on a faraway look, as though she were traveling back through all those years. "Of course, I barely knew you before your mother got sick," she began. "So I can't say what you were like then, but the things I remember most are your energy and your determination. You were so convinced that everything would work out. That you could care for your mother and your sisters and keep the house and still have time for school and friends. I remember overhearing my parents saying that your father was relying on you too much, that he was taking advantage of you. I don't know when you changed. I guess it was so gradual that I just didn't notice. You stopped trying to have friends or dates. You dropped out of all the activities. Sometimes you didn't even come to classes. Everyone missed you and felt bad."

"Did they?" Paige asked.

"Sure! You had a lot of people who liked you."

"I don't remember it that way," Paige said.

"I'm not surprised," Judy said. "After you became so sad and worn out and resigned, you didn't have any friends left, but it didn't start out that way. My parents called it a crime. Said your father ought to be locked up."

Judy sighed and then brightened. "Anyway, the past is gone and you look like everything's terrific now. And I have to confess I have a deep-down selfish reason for being glad to see you doing so well. I felt like such a heel when my family moved and I had to leave you. And then I couldn't even afford to fly back for your mother's funeral. I've felt guilty all these years...."

"And I felt guilty because I couldn't afford to go to your wedding!" Paige said. "Then when I saw you and your husband briefly that time, I...well, I thought you were upset with me for not being able to make it."

"Is that why you stopped writing?" Judy asked.

Paige nodded.

"I thought you were cold toward me because I'd deserted you when you most needed a friend."

Paige was astonished. How could two old friends have had such a lack of communication?

"Should we wail and cry for a while?" Judy asked in mock seriousness.

"Let's save it for later," Paige said, laughing.

She herself had changed, but Judy was just as she'd remembered her. Maybe the sandy hair was a little tamer, the freckles weren't so riotous and the hips were a little broader—a two-baby body, Judy called it—but her spirit was the same. Her bright hazel eyes were still as lively and full of laughter. Her light-hearted attitude toward life and her ready sense of humor were still intact.

Paige could remember yearning for those identical traits, hoping something of her friend would rub off on her. She felt that same wistful yearning even now. Only now she was a realist. Now she knew that she was stuck with what she was. She was a mature woman now. Her personality was fixed, and there was no going back to that time in life when it could have been changed.

Judy kept insisting, until finally Paige recounted the sketchy details of her life. She managed to come up with a few stories about getting her little sisters through high school and finally settled into college that were amusing in an ironic way. Finally she described her father's remarriage. Judy was the only person in the world who knew her and her relationship with her father well enough to appreciate all the emotions stirred up by that ordeal.

"And how's your love life?" Judy probed, never one for subtlety. "Mine's obvious, so it's only fair you spill the beans about yours."

"There's not much to tell," Paige said apologetically.

"Come on," Judy said with a scowl.

"All right, all right. But there's no one special. I have a few men friends. Now and then I go out to dinner or a movie with one of them."

Judy's look was deadly.

"I did have someone last year," Paige admitted reluctantly. "We dated off and on for about eight months, but then he was transferred to New York."

"Did you ever think about marrying him?"

Paige shrugged. "Not seriously. We discussed what it would be like to be married, but it simply wouldn't have been convenient for either of us. Maybe if we had both stayed in the same town we might eventually have reached an understanding."

"God, how practical and unemotional can you get! Where does the love and romance enter into it?" Judy demanded.

"I'm too old for romance," Paige said. "Romance is for the young and naive. It's for people who haven't learned the realities of life yet. And as for love... Sometimes I wonder if I even know how to love, or if maybe all the love I had inside me was drained out by my family. I find it hard even to get close to people to make friends, much less to love. And besides, love isn't a cure-all. Loyalty and responsibility and a sense of duty are enough to make a marriage work."

"Oh, Paige, that's just not true! Look at me. I'm married and raising kids and functioning in the real world, and I have love and romance. In fact, I don't think I could face the realities, the responsibilities and duties, without all that love."

"Maybe things are just different with you," Paige said.

"You say that as if I'm unique! I'm not. Love is out there. Romance is out there. Granted, it's not easy to find, but it is there. Sure it's hard to recognize sometimes, and it's a lot of work figuring it all out and nurturing it along, but it's there, and it's what life is all about."

"Maybe," Paige said, shifting her position on the big bed.

She said the word only to placate her friend. There were no maybes. She knew that her life had gone past the point where romance was possible, and that vague emotion called love was best suited to songs and stories.

"Don't you ever get lonely?" Judy asked, hazel eyes full of concern.

"Sometimes," Paige admitted. "But I've developed ways of cheering myself up. A good book or a chinese dinner, and everything's okay again. And I belong to an organization that helps children. I have a twelve-year-old, Trisha, who's assigned to me. Once a week we do something together. She wanted to come with me on this assignment. I don't know where she got it, but she had some kind of crazy idea that Denver was wonderful."

"Any place can be wonderful," Judy said softly. "It's all in how you see it, and maybe who you see it with. Oh, Paige," she said, sighing. "When are you going to loosen up and have some fun in your life. When are you going to stop being so damn responsible and serious and...and...kick up your heels a little!"

There was that word again—*fun*. Why did everyone think she had no "fun" in her life?

"I have fun," she countered defensively.

"You don't even know what it is!" Judy said. "You've got so much courage and spirit. God knows a lesser person would never have been able to handle what you did and end up as a beautiful, intelligent, all-around good person. But you've still got a lot to learn. Everything you do is so calculated and reasonable. Have you ever done anything impulsive or crazy?" Judy's face lit up as she rushed on. "You know, like F. Scott and Zelda. Remember how Miss Emmers read that piece to the class about Zelda wading in a fountain in New York. Have you ever done anything like that?"

"Certainly not," Paige replied. "Have you?"

"More than once!" Judy announced with a devilish grin.

There was a moment of silence between them. A gap that couldn't be bridged.

"All this talk has made me hungry," Paige said, reaching for the phone. "I'm going to order us both some ice cream from room service. Remember all the ice cream we used to eat together?"

"I can't," Judy wailed, indicating her hips.

"Shush," Paige ordered. "All I want to hear is chocolate or vanilla." She spun the dial on the phone. "Now who says I don't do crazy impulsive things?"

"Okay," Judy giggled. "Chocolate. But I don't know how you do it. Look at you. How can you have a shape like that and eat ice cream? Never mind. Don't even tell me. I'm just destined to look like this."

The remainder of the afternoon was spent discussing rodeo, with Paige an eager student of the sport. The more she learned, the more she admired the men and women she had come to write about. That is, all but one of them.

Several times she started to tell Judy about her experience with Casey Cavanaugh, but it was simply too hard to put it all into words. Maybe later, when she had it in better perspective, maybe then she could share it with her friend.

All too soon the afternoon was over. Paige had an appointment with a livestock contractor to learn more about the care and treatment of the high-priced bucking horses and bulls, and Judy needed to meet Ken. They parted with warmth and the mutual agreement that the following night she would join the couple for dinner out.

Casey had no trouble finding Ken Reynolds in the hotel. They exchanged greetings and information about the animals they had drawn to compete on.

"Say, I met a woman the other night," Casey mentioned casually. "Said she had a married, bull-riding friend from Utah, and I was wondering if it was you. Her name's Bannister. Paige Bannister."

"Sure," Ken said. "Only she's a friend of my wife's, not mine. Matter of fact, the three of us are supposed to go out to dinner tomorrow night."

"I didn't exactly put my best foot forward with her when I met her," Casey admitted, "and I'm kinda lookin' for another shot. I'd ask her out, but I know she'd turn me down."

"Yeah," Ken sympathized, "she's a damn fine lady, but talk about uptight—whew! I can't see even you lightin' a fire under that lady's burner, Case."

Casey shrugged nonchalantly. "I'd still like to see her again," he said. "You know...give it one more go."

Ken rubbed his forehead in thought a moment. "Just come with us!" he suddenly declared. "You can meet us at the restaurant, have a chance to get acquainted over dinner, and then you can drive her back to the hotel. It'll save me a trip, cause Judy and I are goin' dancing after dinner, and we were gonna have to take Paige back before we went. What do you say?"

"Sounds good to me," Casey declared, slapping him on the back. "Only lets keep this just between you and me. Make it a surprise, okay?"

"Sure," Ken agreed. "Whatever you say, Case."

## Chapter Three

Paige answered the door with her hairbrush in her hand. It was Judy, of course. Fifteen minutes early.

"Ready?" Judy asked as soon as the door was open.

"Almost," Paige assured her. "You're early."

"A little," Judy said nervously.

Paige moved to the mirror and began to twist her long hair into a knot.

"Oh, leave it down," Judy insisted. "Come on, you're all dressed and everything. Just leave it down and let's go."

"It'll bother me when I'm eating if I let it just hang," Paige said.

"Just pull back the sides, then. It's so sexy when it's down."

"And why on earth would I want to look sexy?" Paige asked incredulously.

"Don't be difficult," Judy ordered. "Just leave it down and come on!"

Paige shook her head at her friend's strange behavior and pulled each side of her hair back with an antique comb, as a concession. "Does that meet with your approval?" she asked.

"Great!" Judy exclaimed. "You look terrific. Absolutely, positively, wonderfully terrific!"

Paige glanced at herself in the mirror. Her hair looked far too youthful down, in her opinion. And the dress she had on was nice—a muted green georgette with soft ruffles at the wrists and throat—but it was nothing to get silly over. All told, she thought she looked presentable, but certainly nothing more. Why was Judy acting so crazy?

"What are you so keyed up about?" Paige asked as she gathered up her purse and her heavy wool coat.

Judy toyed with the gathers on her black velvet skirt and gave a short laugh. "I'd never dare wear this if the kids were here," she said. "They'd have it decorated with peanut butter and jelly."

Paige waited.

"Someone is joining us for dinner," Judy said weakly.

"Male or female?" Paige demanded.

"A friend of Ken's. His idol really. Ken invited him. I swear I had nothing to do with it." Judy drew in a deep breath and then continued in a more normal speaking voice. "Who knows...you might even think he's interesting. He's smart like you and he's nice, and he's dynamite to look at. In fact," she grinned and raised her eyebrows, "If I weren't a happily married woman..."

"Judy, I refuse to go on a blind date," Paige said firmly.

"It's not a blind date! You promised you'd go to dinner with Ken and me tonight. I can't help it if someone else is coming. Don't be stubborn and ruin everything."

Paige drew in a deep, disapproving breath. "I'll go ... but I don't like it."

"It'll be fine. Trust me," Judy said, pulling open the door. "I personally guarantee you'll have a super good time tonight."

They started down the wide, thickly carpeted hallway. Through the windows the lights of Denver airport glittered in the clear night air.

"All right," Paige said grudgingly, "tell me about him."

"Nope," Judy said with a gleam in her eye. "He's not like anyone you've ever met—and the rest you'll have to find out for yourself. Besides, Ken told me to keep quiet. I shouldn't even have told you he was coming, but I knew how mad you'd be if I didn't."

Paige shook her head and sighed in exasperation.

"I'm not happy about this. Not happy at all."

"Oh, Paige, loosen up! Just try to have a little fun will ya ... for me?"

The drive to the restaurant went quickly. Ken told bad jokes, which Judy hissed and booed at, and Judy told good jokes, but managed to mix up the punch lines. Paige couldn't remember when she had laughed so much.

Ken turned the corner on East Colfax and asked for help in finding the place, Mataam Fez, in the 4600 block. He passed it once and had to backtrack, and there was much good-natured arguing between the couple as to whose fault it was.

"What kind of place is this?" Paige asked as they headed for the door.

"Don't ask me," Ken put in quickly, "and if it's bad, remember, I didn't know anything about it."

"Be quiet, Reynolds," Judy said, and gave him a playful shove. Turning to Paige, she explained it was a Moroccan restaurant that had sounded exciting.

Upon stepping into the tiny entryway, they were surrounded by heavy, deep red draperies.

"Whatever happened to regular old doors and walls?" Ken whispered, and then grunted as Judy elbowed him in the ribs.

"Greetings," an accented voice said, "and welcome to Mataam Fez. May I take your coats?" He emerged fully from behind some draperies, and Paige saw that the disembodied voice belonged to a dark man in flowing, ornate robes and Eastern hat. With great courtesy he ushered them into another small area that was filled with coats and shoes.

"Are we supposed to take off our shoes?" Judy asked in awe.

"As you wish," the man answered. "Many find it more comfortable that way."

Judy giggled and immediately began unbuckling the tiny straps on her shoes. Paige shrugged in answer to Ken's disbelieving look and followed suit. Ken watched them a moment, groaned and began tugging at a camel-colored ostrich-hide boot.

"I hope my socks match," he said dryly as he pulled the second boot off. Then to the dark man he said, "We have a reservation for four in the name of Reynolds—unless I have to take anything else off."

"And another person is meeting us," Judy added.

"Yeah, whenever another guy in a cowboy hat wanders in he'll probably be ours, so send him over."

The berobed man nodded and smiled and beckoned for the three to follow him through yet another set of draperies.

"Wow," Judy exclaimed.

As Paige stepped through the drapes behind Judy she breathed in an exotic, spicy fragrance. The lighting was dim, and it took her eyes a moment to adjust. The room was not overly large, compared to other restaurants she had been in, but that was the only comparison she could make to other restaurants. This was like stepping into another world.

The ceiling was done entirely in draped cloth that extended to the edges and hung down in graceful scallops. It gave her the feeling of being in a huge tent. The deep rich hues of emerald and burgundy and gold were everywhere in the form of tapestries and Oriental rugs. Lining the sides of the room were low round tables of intricately inlaid wood. Surrounding each table were squashy overstuffed pillows and cushions.

She followed the others quietly to a corner table.

"Something tells me we don't get to sit in chairs," Ken mumbled in a low tone.

Paige tried to maintain her dignity as she sat down, but it was next to impossible. She felt embarrassment and regret at having come for a moment, but the feelings passed as soon as Judy joined the struggle. Together they half climbed, half fell into position between the table and the wall. Chuckling, they fished under the table for their pillows, which had been pushed out of place during their none-too-graceful performance, and then spent several hilarious moments shoving the pillows under one another in the close confines.

"Very funny," Ken said, still standing and eyeing the pillow beside Judy with distrust.

"Come on! We left the easy seats on the outside for you guys," Judy told him. "All you have to do is sit down on this thing. Besides, if you can sit on a bull, you can damn sure manage this nice, soft, safe pillow."

Ken gave a sigh of defeat and plunked himself unceremoniously down. "We'd better order a bottle, ladies. I can tell one glass of anything won't be enough tonight."

Wine was poured. There was another bout of good-natured kidding, and Paige felt herself relaxing, letting go, losing herself in the warmth and spirit of the evening. It was a pleasant sensation, but one that was almost foreign to her. She glanced at the empty pillow to her left and hoped Ken's friend wouldn't show up. The moment he did the evening would change for her. She would have to put her guard back up. Regain control. Act sensible and mature.

There was only one other table occupied at the

time, and a waiter was serving after-dinner tea to the group. Paige and her friends watched in amazement as the waiter placed the small, empty glasses behind him on a tray, raised the ornate silver pot high and poured the boiling liquid backward without spilling a drop. He repeated this until all six glasses were full.

"Lord, I wonder how he serves the steak," Ken remarked.

In the midst of a gale of laughter Ken suddenly jumped and waved. *He's here,* Paige thought with dismay. She glanced over her shoulder briefly and saw nothing more than a shadowy form in a big hat. She turned back to look at Judy and Ken, faces wreathed in wide, welcoming smiles, and tried to manufacture a smile on her own face. Again she looked in the direction of the approaching form. He was more distinct in the dim light as he moved closer. Now there was something disturbingly familiar about him. The contrived smile faded from her lips. It couldn't be! It just couldn't be!

Quickly she ducked her head, resting her elbow on the table and holding her forehead with her palm. It wasn't happening. It was just not possible. Her eyes were playing tricks on her.

As if in a nightmare she heard Judy's voice ring out with, "Casey! You made it!"

Her hair was down. That was the first thing Casey noticed as he reached the table. It hung in waves like heavy silk. Just as beautiful as he'd imagined it would be. He couldn't see her face very well. She was looking straight down at the table. He could tell she was angry, though, and he felt suddenly uncertain.

Judy carried on brightly, "Say hello to my friend Paige and grab that pillow beside her."

There was a stirring and bustling as Casey was seated and the waiter was summoned for more wine.

"Ken said he thought you two had run across each other somewhere already," Judy said. "Is that right?"

"Yes," Casey answered quietly. "At the press party the other night."

He was acutely aware of her closeness. She was only inches away. Close enough to touch. He could smell her perfume. He could see her chest rising and falling. He felt gripped by something totally unexplainable, something beyond his understanding or experience.

"Oh, yeah," Judy was saying. "One of those circuses. No one can ever really get acquainted at one of those things."

"What?" Casey asked.

"Press parties," Judy said.

Paige had not said a word.

"Come on, Paige. Join the party!" Judy coaxed. "You can at least say hi. Casey's harmless."

"Is he?" Paige said.

Her voice sounded strange.

"Sure," Judy said, eyeing Paige quizzically. "A little intimidating, maybe, but that's all."

To his surprise, Paige turned her head and looked straight at him. Her eyes were cool and wary. He imagined it was the same look she also gave to snakes and poisonous spiders.

"I don't find him the least bit intimidating," Paige said evenly.

Casey searched for something to say. Anything.

"How's your work going?" he pulled out of the air.

"Quite well," she answered shortly.

"I'm amazed you had time to go out like this. I figured you were always working," he teased gently.

"I am," she said. "In fact, the most innocent of occasions can turn into work." She picked up her glass of wine, held it up as though studying the liquid's colour and shot him a fiery sideways glance. "But, then, you're quite a worker yourself, aren't you?"

"Oh, he is!" Judy chimed in innocently. "He works hard at everything he does. And he's good, too—at everything."

Paige smiled a cat-eating-the-mouse smile. "Not even a few minor failures hidden away?" she asked brightly.

"Not Casey," Judy said with a laugh, unaware of any undertones. "He doesn't have even minor failures!"

Casey managed a weak smile. "How's your assignment coming?" he asked Paige in an effort to steer the conversation elsewhere.

"I've still got a lot to learn about the sport," Paige said.

"You'll be an unquestioned authority in no time," Judy assured her.

"You mean a questionable authority," Paige said.

"No!" Judy protested, and then turned to Casey. "She was completely new to rodeo, and you wouldn't believe how fast she's picking things up."

"A quick learner," Casey remarked.

"And like an elephant," Paige said. "Once I've learned something I never forget it."

"Do you already know about Casey, Paige?" Judy

asked eagerly. "He's really famous. He's broken every record ever set in the riding events." Judy's eyes twinkled mischievously. "All that, and he's available, too!"

Casey winced inwardly at her choice of words. Poor Judy. She had no inkling of trouble. He noticed that Ken, on the other hand, had caught on to the undercurrents.

"Yes, I realize he's famous—or infamous, maybe," Paige said, glancing at him briefly. "And I think his availability must be legendary."

"Yup," Judy continued blissfully on. "He always has fans after him."

"I understand it's very tiring to constantly have someone after you," Paige put in, glaring briefly at him.

Casey lost himself in her eyes for a moment. Word games. How he hated word games. But he would play. It was worth it just to hear her voice, look at her. A ridiculous line from an old Western popped into his head. *"You shore are purty when you get mad."* What a stupid, condescending thing for a man to say to a woman. But now, watching this woman beside him, he was tempted to say the same dumb thing. Her cheeks were burning and her eyes were flashing green sparks, and she was damned sure beautiful when she was angry!

"It's not tiring so much as it is tiresome," he said in reply to her disdainful comment.

She looked faintly surprised, but recovered her anger quickly. "That's a terrible attitude. How would your 'fans' feel if they heard you say that?"

"My 'fans' aren't interested in anything I have to

say. They're only interested in how I perform."

"And most of your 'performances' are successful, I take it. How proud you must be."

Tension crackled in the air.

Casey chose his words carefully, slowly. "Sometimes," he began, "a person isn't necessarily proud of what he's successful at."

"Baloney!" Judy cut in. "You ought to be proud of everything you've done!"

"Oh-oh!" Ken said loudly, and made a show of examining his watch. "It's time to call the kids. Remember, honey, we promised we'd call home at eight sharp tonight."

He jumped up and reached for Judy's arm. She looked at him blankly and started to speak.

"Nope," he cut her off firmly. "No arguments about how expensive it is. We just won't talk long."

He pulled her to her feet and ushered her away from the table at top speed.

Casey drew in a deep breath and studied Paige. They were alone now, and she was obviously uncomfortable. She stared across the room at Judy's and Ken's retreating backs.

"It's just you and me now. You can stop pretending to be civil and say whatever you want," he said.

The look she gave him was pure fire.

"All right," she snapped. "I cannot believe that even you were low enough to pull this. Of all the sneaky, manipulative tricks. What did you think you'd accomplish? Did you think I'd change my mind about you if I saw you across a table? Did you think the sight of you eating would fool me into believing you're a decent human being?"

"You sure are pretty when you get mad," he said, unable to resist using the line a minute longer.

Her expression went through several stages of disbelief, then on to rage and finally back to garden-variety anger.

"You're insane," she said. "And I refuse to stay in the same room with you."

He watched her struggling to slide out from behind the table. Floundering among the pillows made her madder and madder. He fought to keep a straight face.

"You can't just leave," he said. "You'll ruin Judy and Ken's evening."

She froze and glared at him. "Me! You're the one who's ruined everything! You're the one who's at fault, not me."

"All right," he admitted, feeling suddenly guilty. "I knew you were going to be here, and I probably shouldn't have come. I thought..." He shrugged.

"You thought," she said, "you could use Judy and Ken. Some friend you must be. You thought you could force yourself on me one more time and I would be swept away by your 'irresistible charms.' You thought you could manipulate everyone and everything around you until you got your way. Well, you thought wrong!"

"I deserve all that," he said quietly.

It was ironic. He attracted so many women. His friends kidded him about it constantly. He never had to try. He never had to work at it. He hadn't "chased" after a girl since high school. In fact, he spent the majority of his time devising ways to avoid this female or that. And now, now that he had finally found a woman he wanted, suddenly nothing was working. He couldn't seem to do anything right. And the harder he tried the worse he looked to her.

"I won't bother you again," he said, and meant it.

He knew what it was like to be the object of unwanted attention. How often had he been pursued by women with amorous intentions that he not only didn't share, but was revolted by? How often had he been pursued until his indifference escalated into dislike and finally disgust?

Never, never would he let himself sink to such a level. He had too much pride to continue after a woman who so obviously disliked him. He would accept his defeat like a gentleman and hope that somewhere in this wide world was another woman who could attract and excite him as this woman did, that somewhere in the world was a woman he could love.

"I was wrong," he said quietly. "Wrong about everything."

Her eyes were on him, no longer full of anger but now guarded and unreadable. He could get lost in those eyes. He took a deep breath and ran his fingers roughly through his hair. Anything to distract himself from those eyes.

"It's clear that neither one of us can just get up and leave," he said shortly. "That would kill the Reynolds's evening just as surely as anything. And unless you have another solution—" he paused giving her a chance to speak, but she kept silent "—then we're both stuck at this table for the duration, and I'm not any happier about it than you are. All we can do is sit

it out and try to act like we're enjoying ourselves...
and when this is over, I promise you won't be bothered by me again."

Paige felt incredibly guilty. She realized she'd been
acting like a selfish child and not considering the feelings of her friends. The last thing she wanted was to
make Judy unhappy. In short, she'd allowed herself
to sink to Casey's level.

Why was he being so civil and polite about everything? Why was he admitting he was wrong? He was
probably trying a different strategy, a different plan of
attack. Even realizing that, it was still hard to stay mad
at someone who was being so damned reasonable!

Why did he have to be here at all? He looked so
good in that starched, white shirt. His hat was off and
his dark, wavy hair looked soft and clean. He turned
to watch the Reynoldses return, and she let her gaze
wander from the small scar on his temple to the
chiseled line of his jaw.

She felt suddenly frightened, almost panicky. She
picked up her wineglass and drank till it was empty.

As soon as Ken and Judy were seated Casey took
charge. He assured them that everything had been "resolved." He summoned the waiter for menus, had
everyone's wineglass refilled and complimented Judy
on her lace blouse.

Judy beamed, and Paige knew that the evening was
on the mend. Thus far it had all been Casey's doing.
Paige wanted to make a gesture of her own. Something to atone for her previous behavior.

"A toast," she announced with manufactured enthusiasm. "To good friends...and good food...hopefully!"

Everyone was quick to raise their glass in response. Casey touched his glass to hers with a fathomless look in his dark eyes, and she drank nervously and deeply again, draining the pale wine as quickly as it had been poured.

The restaurant's unusual character made it easy to maintain a festive mood. Patiently the waiter explained the foreign menu. They all laughed over Casey's order of *lièvre 'M Hammer,* which turned out to be rabbit. He laughed with them but stuck with his choice. Ken chose *brochette de veau,* which was veal, and Judy kidded him about never ordering anything but "cow meat." Judy elected to try *couscous aux mouton,* which was a lamb dish, and finally Paige ordered *poulet k'dra aux miel,* a combination of chicken with honey and almonds, which sounded intriguing.

There was a great deal of ceremony included in the meal. Big silver bowls were brought and warm water was poured over their hands. They were then presented with fluffy towels, and Ken made a crack about the towels being the same thing they used as napkins for the kids at home.

The first courses to be brought out were on single large dishes and were placed in the center of the table. The waiter explained that they were all to eat out of the same dish, and utensils would be furnished only if they demanded them. The traditional method of eating was with one's fingers. This brought about much laughter and various jokes about a host of communicable diseases that might necessitate banning someone from the communal dish.

Hesitantly Paige dipped her fingers into the chilled mixture of tomatoes and spices and finely chopped eggplant before her. It was wonderful! She reached for more at the same time Casey did. Their hands touched. A current of lightning shot through her body. How would she ever make it through the night? She downed more wine and smiled brightly at no one in particular.

A huge, round pastry filled with meat and cinnamon was presented next. She gauged her eating. Never reach for anything when Casey was reaching. She joined in the exclamations over each course, and she forced herself to join in the laughter. Her wineglass was refilled again and again.

"Oh, take it away," Judy moaned, holding her stomach as if she were in pain and pushing her plate toward the center of the table.

Paige heard Judy's declaration and the teasing that followed. She heard Ken's threat to lay down on his pillow, instead of sitting on it. She heard the laughter about finding room for the dessert pastries and tea. But it was all vague and far away. She wasn't touched by it. None of this was happening to her.

"You're quiet, Paige. Too full to talk?" Judy asked.

Paige turned her head to look at her friend, but couldn't quite focus. Judy's face was fuzzy. She opened and shut her eyes several times in her efforts.

"You all right?" Judy asked.

"Sure," Paige said, and finished off another glass of wine.

"The kids would get a big kick out of all this," Judy said, glancing around the room. "Course if they were here, we wouldn't be enjoying it!"

"I heard that!" Ken said in a declaration of agreement. "Specially poor ole Case here. Whenever they see him they get wild and want to crawl all over him."

Casey laughed. "It's not completely their fault," he said. "I enjoy all that wrestling around, too."

"Bet your Trisha would get a bang out of this, Paige," Judy said, obviously attempting to draw Paige into the conversation.

"Who's that?" Ken asked.

Paige could feel everyone's eyes on her, waiting for her to answer. She tried to formulate a suitable response, something that would explain briefly and simply. Nothing came to her. Finally she just said, "A little friend of mine." "Little" came out lacking its ts. Paige toyed with her empty wineglass until Ken reached over and refilled it, and then she sipped, wishing they would change the subject and shift the attention away from her.

"Oh!" Judy said, voice full of exasperation. "Trisha's not just a lil' friend of Paige's. My stubborn 'big' friend is just being humble again. Trisha is an underprivileged twelve-year-old whom Paige has taken on in some kind of a big sister program. The idea is that Paige spends time with the child every week and offers her guidance and affection and whatever. I'll bet she's good at it, too. She had lots of experience raising her own two sisters."

"That's great," Ken said.

"You should be proud of that," Casey said in a voice that was much too close for comfort.

"Watch this guy," she heard Ken whisper to Casey as the waiter brought their after-dinner tea. She was

emotion, not logic or reason. Reality consisted solely of how she felt right now, this minute.

"Dance with me," she said, and held her arms out.

He studied her a moment, then laid his coat on the dresser and reached out for her hand. She moved into his arms easily. It felt so perfect, resting her head on his shoulder, eyes closed, swaying to music that wasn't there. He smelled like sunshine and new leather. His crisp, pressed shirt felt good against her cheek. She moved in closer to him.

"That's enough," he said gruffly, pulling away. "I need to go."

She turned quickly and had to grab hold of a chair to keep from falling. The room spun crazily around her. "I feel funny," she said weakly.

His strong arms closed around her. She shut her eyes and leaned against him, supremely content, coasting on all the pleasant sensations his nearness brought. She didn't realize he was maneuvering her toward the bed until she sat down on it.

"I'm not sleepy," she said, her words fuzzy.

He ignored her and bent to take off her shoes. His hands looked so big, struggling with the tiny buckles.

"What do you sleep in?" he asked, looking around the room.

She tried to tell him, but it came out as a mumble.

He crossed the room, and she could hear him in the bathroom, looking. *It's not in there,* she thought, *it's in the drawer.* But she didn't really care whether he found the nightgown or not. Her pillow looked very inviting. She let herself melt sideways onto the bed.

"You can't sleep in that dress," she heard him say.

"I'm going to leave, and I want you to get up and take that dress off."

She could hear him, but she couldn't seem to open her eyes or say anything. Of course she would take her dress off. She'd never sleep in her dress.

"Oh, hell," she heard him mutter.

She felt a tugging at her belt and then heard the sound of a zipper. She was pulled back into a sitting position and the dress was yanked roughly over her head. She opened her eyes and looked down at herself. The satin of her slip gleamed in the dim light. She saw Casey hanging up her dress. She watched his shirt pull across the muscles of his arms and shoulders. She watched the lean, hard line of his thighs move beneath the cloth of his trousers.

He walked toward her, and she felt a stirring deep inside, a series of sensations she had never known before. She felt like a lit fuse. One throbbing point of warmth— burning, burning toward some cataclysmic explosion.

Casey moved across the room toward her. The shimmering slip clung to her body, detailing every curve. One strap slipped down, partially revealing the swell of her breast. Her hair had fallen loose and hung like a heavy silk curtain, shadowing her eyes, tumbling over her smooth shoulders. She held out her arms to him and he thought he would die of wanting her.

He knew he could take her now if he chose. Take her with little or no protest. Knew he could put his mouth on the perfect line of her throat and bury his face in that sweet smelling hair. Knew he could put his hands on the swell of her breasts and the curve of her hips. Knew he could crush her to him, losing himself in her softness.

It would be easy. She was so fuzzy with wine she would barely know what was happening. The wine was the sole reason for her acquiescence. The wine had mellowed and softened her. But it hadn't changed her opinion of him. He was certain of that. He still didn't stand a chance with a sober Paige Bannister. And if he did take advantage of her he would be proving that every bad thing she thought about him was true. He would be acting just like the disgusting man she thought him to be.

Still, knowing all of this, knowing with absolute certainty that he could never make love to her under these circumstances, didn't make the aching, the physical wanting, stop.

He pushed her reaching hands away, took hold of her shoulders and laid her gently down. He pulled the blanketes free and drew them up around her.

"Don't go yet," she said.

She was like a child, wanting to be tucked in, cuddled and talked to at bedtime. It didn't surprise him. He'd seen a lot of people become children when they drank too much.

"I'm tired," he said.

"Not fair," she moaned, throwing one bare arm across her eyes.

"What?" he asked.

"You, everywhere."

So she was still worried that she wasn't rid of him.

"Don't worry," he said harshly, "I'll be out of your life as of tomorrow."

She seemed not to have heard. She was mumbling, talking more to herself than to him.

"Not s'posed to feel this way...don't wanna feel this way...you're bad."

"I know you think I'm bad," he said wearily. "Now I've got to go."

She lowered her arm and looked at him. "Kiss me," she said.

He shook his head no and turned to leave.

"Please," she said, "a good-night kiss."

He bent over, intending to kiss her lightly on the cheek, but she wound her arms around his neck and pulled him down, her lips hungry on his.

Fire spread through his loins and he gave himself to the kiss, to the moment. Then awareness struck, and he drew back sharply, pulling free of her arms.

"Please," she said, "please." And he heard it in her voice, saw it in her eyes—she wanted him, too!

"You don't know what you're saying," he cautioned her. "It's just the wine talking. Tomorrow you'd hate yourself, not to mention me."

"Don't care 'bout tomorrow," she said, and for a moment he almost believed her.

"Yes, you do," he told her, brushing a strand of hair from her cheek. "You didn't want me yesterday and you won't want me tomorrow. Tonight is just..."

"I did," she said.

"Did what?"

"Did want you yesterday," she said, her words fading and fuzzy.

"No, you didn't."

She nodded sleepily and shut her eyes.

"You're all wrong," she mumbled. "Wrong kind of man. Bad man. Wrong to want you. Can't help it. Just want to..."

Her words faded and she drifted into sleep. He sat on the edge of the bed, watching her, thinking. He'd had some experience with drinking women. They usually didn't say anything when they were giddy that hadn't been on their minds when they were sober. Alcohol certainly didn't cause them to suddenly want a man whom they loathed when they were sober. Sure, he knew that a fellow could force himself on a woman under the influence fairly easily, but that wasn't the same thing. He hadn't been forcing himself on her. She had wanted him! She had felt the pull of desire just as he had. And if she was that attracted to him now, that must mean she felt something for him when she was sober, too, regardless of all their misunderstandings.

His heart soared. He still had a chance. He had more than a chance! If he could just break through that icy reserve of hers. If he could just show her what kind of a man he really was. If he could prove to her that she'd been wrong... He felt like jumping and shouting.

The ski trip tomorrow! He hadn't planned on going, but he could ask to see the reservation list. If her name was on it nothing could keep him from getting on that plane!

She roused, opened her eyes and mumbled something.

"I'm going now," he said. "Will you be comfortable sleeping like that?"

She mumbled again. He leaned close to hear her.

"Oh, no!" he said with a laugh. "You're out of luck if you want me to do that tonight!"

She mumbled something in protest, but he was already halfway to the door.

The sound wouldn't go away. Paige drifted slowly into awareness. The sound was knocking. She turned on the bedside lamp and checked her watch. Six o'clock in the morning! Was this some kind of joke. The knocking continued.

She answered the door cautiously. It was room service. The tray held orange juice and hot tea, fresh warm doughnuts and a newspaper, and a single, red rose in a vase.

She fumbled in her purse for money.

"Oh, no, miss," the uniformed man assured her. "It's already been taken care of ... tip and all."

"When?" she asked in disbelief.

The man consulted a slip of paper. "Late last night," he said.

Paige felt awful. She downed the cold juice quickly. Her throat was dry, her head hurt and her eyes were scratchy. Was she coming down with something? She couldn't remember ever feeling so wrung out.

The phone shrilled loudly. Paige held her head with one hand and lifted the receiver with the other.

"Good, I caught you," Judy's voice said.

"Caught me what?" Paige asked, still holding her head.

"Caught you before you went down."

"Down?"

"C'mon, Paige. Wake up. This morning's the ski trip."

"Ohhhhh," Paige groaned.

"Bet you're not feeling too perky this morning. You put enough wine away to down a world-class drinker, and since you're not even used to it..."

Paige groaned again. Wine. That was why she felt so terrible. She had a hangover!

"Oh, Judy, I'm so embarrassed. I don't know what happened...I just..."

"Don't be silly," Judy cut in. "There's nothing to be embarrassed about. You're not exactly a problem drinker, and you weren't driving. I was glad to see you relax and loosen up for a change."

"I can't even remember going to bed," Paige wailed.

"Don't worry about it," Judy ordered. "You were among friends. Now the important thing is for you to take a couple of aspirin and pull yourself together for the ski trip. There'll be a lot of great material for your story, and you don't want to miss it. In fact, I guess it's a good thing I called and woke you up."

"I was already awake," Paige said. "Room service came knocking this morning with a big tray, and I don't remember even ordering it. I must have been totally out of it last night."

"You probably didn't order it," Judy said. "Last night Casey asked me what kind of juice you liked and whether you drank coffee or tea. I'll bet it was him."

Casey. The name brought her fully awake. Casey had been in her room last night!

"Anyway," Judy was saying, "the reason I called

was to tell you Ken and I aren't going to make it today. He's up on his bull tonight, and he's worried
something might happen and we won't make it back.
Can't blame him, I guess. I remember one year when
nobody made it back to Denver till the next day.''

Paige agreed with her and said all the appropriate
things about seeing her later, et cetera, but her mind
wasn't on the conversation. Her mind was on Casey
Cavanaugh. Casey Cavanaugh in this room. Casey
Cavanaugh pulling her dress off. Casey Cavanaugh
bending over the bed, kissing her. God, what had she
done!

She covered her face with her hands. Had she let him
make love to her last night? Or worse yet had he taken
advantage of her semiconscious state and forced himself upon her?

The more bits and snatches she remembered, the
more she worried about it in her mind, the more certain she became that it had happened. That man had
made love to her in this room last night, either by
persuasion or by actual force. Casey Cavanaugh had
won again.

Now she saw that the room service he'd ordered
was nothing more than a declaration of victory, a slap
in the face. Was he boasting of his conquest right now
to some bunch of cowboys? The thought was so de-
grading, so demeaning, that she was physically sickened by it. She wanted to run away, catch the first
plane back to California. But she couldn't, of course.
She had a responsibility to her company. She had
agreed to do a job and she had to finish it. She swallowed hard against the tightness in the back of her

throat. If the ski trip was important she would be there, one way or another.

Paige pressed her forehead against the cool oval of the window and tried to see the wings and propellers of the plane. It was a big plane, but it wasn't a jet. She wondered vaguely if that made it outdated or unsafe. No matter. She was committed. She wasn't about to get off.

There were still people straggling onto the plane, but Paige ignored them. Outside her window a rabbit darted across the dry winter grass and onto the concrete, where it dodged the sun-sparkled puddles of melted snow. A departing jet hefted its massive bulk, engines roaring, wheels folding inward, and climbed off into the gem-brilliant sky.

She saw everything, but the images went unrecorded. Her mind was drifting, distant.

How had her life come to this? She had always tried so hard to be practical and responsible. To be true to her conscience and her principles. How had she ended up in this situation? How had she become, overnight, both an embarrassing drunk and a cheap lay for some conceited, womanizing cowboy.

The answer was painfully difficult to face, but she knew what it was. Sexual chemistry or animal magnetism or intense physical attraction—whatever the term was. It all amounted to the same thing. Casey Cavanaugh had awakened something within her that she could neither control nor ignore. In trying to shut out the feelings she had turned to alcohol, and that had only compounded the problem. Weakened by wine, all the feelings she had kept harnessed were suddenly unleashed. She knew in her heart that whatever had happened last night had not been against her will. She had wanted him. Under the influence of the wine the attraction she'd felt had turned to immediate need.

She could blame no one but herself. Casey was not the culprit now. It was her own weak will that deserved to be the object of her anger and disgust. How could she have allowed herself to be used in such a way? Or was it she that had used him? Either thought was disturbing. And what must he think of her now?

"Saving this for me?"

The words yanked her coldly back to reality with a sharp intake of breath.

Casey sat down and stretched out his legs as though he owned the spot next to her.

"Have any trouble getting up?" he asked with a look of amusement.

"None," Paige said shortly.

She stood, picking up her coat and purse, and stepped awkwardly over him to get to the aisle. He said nothing, but she could feel his eyes on her. Heart pounding, she headed down the aisle toward the tail. No empty seats. She turned, lifted her chin and headed back up the aisle toward the front. There was not an empty seat on the entire plane! She scanned the sea of cowboy hats, but nowhere in that laughing, chattering mass was there another vacant chair.

Curious eyes stared at her as she walked back to her original place. Did any of them know? Had he bragged to any of them about her? Were any of them looking at her right now and thinking of her as Casey's latest conquest? She felt cheapened and humiliated at the thought. Her face was burning by the time she sat back down beside him.

"Plane's full," he said.

Was that sympathy in his voice?

"Last night at dinner you promised I wouldn't be bothered by you anymore," she said, summoning whatever dignity she had left.

He nodded and looked hard into her face. "That was before... before what happened in your room."

A hot shaft seared through her chest, and she turned her head quickly toward the window. How much did he intend to hurt her with her mistake? How much would he use that moment of weakness against her?

"I prefer to forget last night," she said, staring blindly at the window.

"I can't forget it," he said softly. "And I don't think you can, either."

She looked at him through eyes hot with unshed tears and had the sudden, sinking feeling that she would never be free of Casey Cavanaugh, that he would haunt her forever.

The flight to Steamboat for the cowboy's ski contest was blessedly short. She buried herself in a magazine until landing, pointedly ignoring Casey's presence. He didn't try to talk to her again until time to deplane.

"Let me help you," he said, reaching for her carryon bag.

She clutched her belongings tightly and shook her head, managing only a curt, "No, thanks," in response. The noisy boisterous crowd pressed in tightly around her. She wanted to run, to race off the plane and put as much distance between her and this man as she could, but she could barely move in the press of bodies.

Gradually the crush inched forward and then picked up speed. The plane emptied quickly. She pushed ahead, murmuring apologies, hurrying, trying somehow to escape.

She stumbled, dropping her tote bag. Two hands darted out and steadied her from behind. She whirled around, ready to lash out, certain it was Casey again, but Casey was several feet away. This man was a stranger. A tall, lanky stranger who tipped his hat and said, "Ma'am," as he picked up her tote and handed it to her.

"Thank you," Paige said gratefully.

The man shrugged shyly and gave her one of the most incredibly boyish smiles she'd ever seen. He had sandy-brown hair and brown eyes she would have had to describe as innocent if she'd been pressed to do so.

He fell in beside her easily, matching his long-legged stride to hers.

"I'm Paige Bannister," she told him.

He nodded and tipped his hat again. "My pleasure," he said with a charming drawl. "Name's Scott Cannon."

The man's deferential attitude and obvious respect for her status as a lady made her feel noticeably better about herself. She was not a "groupie" and she never would be. Her self-esteem might be dented, but it was still intact. She would show Casey Cavanaugh that she could rise above last night. That he couldn't so easily defeat her and all she believed in. That she could dismiss it for the mistake it was and pick up with her life where she'd left off.

As she climbed into one of the shuttle vehicles she caught a glimpse of Casey watching her. She settled in next to Scott Cannon with a sense of satisfaction. There were nice men around, and her instincts told her that Scott was one of them. She would make it perfectly clear to Casey Cavanaugh that this was the kind of man she intended to spend her time around—someone who was polite, respectful and unpretentious.

When they arrived at the lodge the shy stranger got out and stood there, offering his hand to help her out. Paige felt a pleasure bordering on smugness. Scott was a perfect example of the kind of man she approved of. She would show Casey Cavanaugh and get rid of him for good!

They started toward the lodge together and the sight nearly took Paige's breath away. The snow was clean and silvery bright in the morning sun. The building itself was invitingly massive, with lots of wood and stone and glass. It was a Christmas card come to life. She looked up and saw a large bird soaring and dipping high in the sky.

"What's that?" she asked breathlessly.

"Looks like an eagle," Scott said.

Paige's spirits soared with the bird. It was an omen. There still were eagles and pure snowy drifts and decent men in the world.

"I've never been on one of these ski trips," she

began tentatively, "and I don't know what the schedule is... but I was wondering if you might have time later to get together with me here at the lodge... for a little informal interview... and maybe a cup of coffee?"

Scott beamed down at her. "That would just be dandy, ma'am, and don't worry 'bout the schedules—I'll just make time."

They reached the doors to the lodge and flowed inside with the crowd. The interior was every bit as impressive as the exterior had been. Everything was on a massive scale, including the fireplace with its cheery, crackling blaze.

The long process of outfitting all the cowboys with ski equipment began, and Paige drifted around, listening to bits and snatches of conversation and absorbing the gaiety and flavor of the day.

The cowboys were different in this environment. She had seen them stilted and relatively subdued—though she hadn't realized it at the time—at the press party. She had seen them serious and intense behind the chutes at the rodeo. She had seen groups of them crazily drinking and showing off for their girls in the hotel lobby.

Now she was seeing yet another side. The general mood was one of exuberant good humor. There was much laughing and joking and teasing. She jotted down notes and observations, constantly aware of Casey's eyes following her every movement.

She was handed a program of the day's events, and she scanned it eagerly. Some basic instruction on the beginner slope for the novices, followed by an afternoon of cowboy ski contests. Then an awards banquet in the evening. She was still reading the program, when someone cleared his throat right next to her. She looked up to find Scott directly in front of her, hat in hand and brown eyes lowered.

"Did you get your equipment all set?" she asked.

"Sure did, ma'am. Since you mentioned us gettin' together later I was wondrin' if you might sit down to lunch with me?"

Paige agreed, and they arranged a meeting place and time.

The morning of instruction passed quickly, with Paige enjoying herself among the friendly, enthusiastic crowd of spectators and press. More than half the cowboys had no notion of how to ski, and the results were hilarious. As lunchtime drew near she started back to the lodge with a group of newspaper photographers.

"How long do you think you can avoid me?"

Paige forced an icy calm into her voice. "What makes you think I've been avoiding you, Casey?"

"It's pretty obvious, lady."

"I haven't been avoiding you," she said evenly, and continued walking. "I haven't even noticed you."

His eyes darkened, and he took hold of her arm and spun her around to face him. "What kind of a game do you think you're playing, Paige?"

"Just leave me alone, Casey Cavanaugh. If I were playing any games they wouldn't include you."

"That's not what you said last night."

She felt the red creep into her cheeks.

"I'm sorry," he said quickly. "When I'm around

you I never seem to say the right things...I...I get so shook up and worried about what you think."

His eyes were so blue, so intense, so sincere. Her chest tightened and her knees grew shaky, and she wanted to lean against him. She wanted to rest her cheek against his soft down jacket and feel his arms around her. Maybe she was wrong about him. Maybe...

"Will you have lunch with me?"

She opened her mouth to answer, but before the words would come, another voice cut into her consciousness.

"Well, howdy, here's my lunch date," Scott announced loudly, and slipped a possessive arm around her waist.

She let herself be led away by Scott, but the look Casey gave her was devastating. There was no anger in it. Nothing to gloat over or feel smug about. It was a look filled with hurt and disappointment.

Nothing was going the way she'd planned it, and now Scott was suddenly coming on a little too possessively for her taste. By the time they were seated in the dining room she was miserable. She couldn't see Casey anywhere.

She still had a job to do. She couldn't lose sight of that. And she had learned that mild-mannered Scott Cannon was quite a well-known calf roper, so she resolved not to think about Casey. She would use this opportunity to get a good story on Cannon and deal with her emotions later.

Scott would have no part of it, though. "Let's just have a relaxin' lunch," he insisted, "and I promise I'll spill my life story soon as the contests are over."

The contests were every bit as wild as Paige had imagined they would be. Cowboys in chaps and hats skiied around barriers and roped girls, or flew down hills crashing into one another, or raced to horses and tried to mount in a flurry of poles and skis. The media had a field day. Cameras whirred and shutters clicked in a continuous background static, drowned only by the occasional shouts and cheers of the spectators. She watched the antics quietly, her mind full of confusion.

Casey came careering down the slope, red chaps flying. He was almost to the finish, when his skis tangled and he went tumbling down in a shower of white. She held her breath. Her heart pounded loudly in her ears.

In less than a minute he was up, grinning and dusting the fine powder from his clothes. Several cowboys ran out to tease him and slap him on the back. He laughed with them and maneuvered his skis around so he could retrieve his hat. He tracked slowly across the finish line, and was instantly surrounded by a clutch of cooing women.

Paige clenched her fists and drew in a deep breath. It was obvious what kind of man he was. Why wasn't she strong enough to wipe him from her mind? She didn't want to be a conquest, another notch on his belt, an object of bragging around the bar. She couldn't live with herself as that kind of person. She couldn't let him make her into that.

She was cold and sick at heart by the time Scott's turn came. He sailed down the slope in perfect form, and she imagined how graceful he must be when roping calves. He was an easy winner.

She left the gaiety and trudged back to the lodge alone. She felt dejected, down, and she didn't want to examine the reasons. She was tired of all the agonizing, tired of the self-searching. She just wanted to get away and forget. Everything would be all right tomorrow. If she could just mark time and keep from thinking till tomorrow came. If she could just stay away from Casey Cavanaugh.

"Been lookin' for ya."

Scott Cannon plunked his lanky form down on the couch beside her.

"Just taking a break," Paige said, and turned so she could study him.

He was undeniably handsome, and he had a guileless charm. He was polite and appealing—everything she'd thought she wanted in a man—but he left her cold. A week ago that wouldn't have mattered. A week ago she hadn't known what it was like to burn inside for a man.

"You won that last race, didn't you?" she asked.

Scott looked down at his boot toes. "Reckon so," he admitted modestly. "You musta brought me luck." He looked back up at her and grinned a dazzling, boyish grin.

Why, Paige asked herself, why couldn't this be the man who made her ache inside? Why couldn't this be the man who filled her dreams and haunted her days? Why did it have to be Casey Cavanaugh? So many decent men in the world and she was attracted to someone like him. There was no sense to it!

"You know, we got some time 'fore the banquet," Scott said, "and you look as tired of all this as I am."

She stared into the fire in silent agreement.

"How 'bout goin' for a snowmobile ride with me?" he asked. "I've got one all lined up." He grinned. "And I'm a good driver."

"Sounds good," she said. In fact, it sounded perfect. A perfect way to shut off her mind and keep away from Casey for the rest of the afternoon.

She climbed on the machine behind Scott, put her arms around his waist, and they roared off into the sparkling whiteness.

Casey was walking back to the lodge in the midst of a good-natured group when he heard the snowmobile engine. He glanced up and couldn't believe what he saw. Scott Cannon and Paige! And they were headed toward nowhere.

He sprinted away from his friends, ignoring their surprised cries. He knew Scott Cannon, knew all of his tricks, knew just what a skunk the man was, and he was determined to find out exactly what Scott was up to. He couldn't allow Paige to become another of Cannon's "victims."

## Chapter Five

The snowmobile flew through the sparkling open meadow and into the light and shadow of the forest. Paige immersed herself in a host of wonderful sensations. The glistening snow against the deep green of the trees. The clean, fresh mountain air, touched with the fragrance of pine. The lulling motion of the machine and the constant drone of the engine.

They stopped by a stream, and Paige marveled over the work of a beaver. Scott broke the ice and she knelt to taste the clear, coldness of the running water underneath. She stood, her eyes sweeping the majestic view around her, and drew in a deep breath. She felt refreshed, renewed, ready to tackle life again. Ready to make some clear-cut decisions and take action. Ready to resolve the Casey Cavanaugh dilemma once and for all.

She would go back to the lodge and find Casey. Then... Then what? She would talk to him, have a shouting match if necessary. Whatever it took. Of course she would give him a chance to say his piece—that was only fair. She'd give him a chance to convince her that his "intentions were honorable." And she had to admit to herself that she wanted to be convinced, that she wanted to be able to give in to all the feelings she had for him.

And if he didn't convince her? Maybe he would do the opposite then. Maybe he would reveal himself to be so disgusting that her desire would finally turn to honest loathing. At least that would be something she could understand and cope with.

She glanced down at her watch and gasped. She'd had no idea how late it was. The afternoon had flown.

"We need to be getting back, Scott. It's almost time for the banquet."

"Well, it sure is, isn't it," he said. "All aboard."

She was anxious now. She couldn't wait to get back and find Casey. She hung on tight to Scott's coat and scanned the horizon eagerly, squinting against the rushing wind. The lodge was nowhere in sight.

"How much longer?" she asked, shouting to be overheard.

"Not long," he answered vaguely.

The snowmobile's engine coughed and sputtered. She held her breath and willed it to keep running.

The sputtering died out and there was silence. They coasted a few feet and then came to a dead stop.

"What is it? What's wrong?" Paige asked.

"Don't know," Scott said, fiddling with the controls.

"Are we out of gas?" she asked.

"Nope, not according to the gauge."

She stood beside Scott and stared at the machine.

"Is it like a car? Could it be something with the battery?"

"Beats me," Scott said, shaking his head. "All I know about is horses and cows."

"Well," Paige said, drawing in a deep breath, "looks like we walk."

"I don't know," Scott said. "That's a pretty good hike through all that deep snow..."

"What other choice do we have?" Paige countered dryly.

It was slow going. There were places where the drifts concealed holes or drop-offs and they each took several tumbles. When the cabin suddenly loomed up through the trees it looked more than inviting.

"We can get help!" Paige cried, and broke into an awkward, leaping run through the snow.

Scott outdistanced her with his long legs, and was opening the door by the time she caught up.

"No one's here," he said. "It looks deserted, but its open."

The cabin looked as though it hadn't been used recently. Paige stood in the center of the large single room and with dismay surveyed the sheet-covered furniture and the dusty stairs to the sleeping loft.

"No help here," she remarked. "Guess it's back to walking."

"Now just wait a minute," Scott said. "There's a big stack of cut wood and a kettle to boil water over the fire. Least we can do is warm ourselves and maybe rustle up some hot coffee or tea or something. Kind of give us a fresh start, you know.''

Paige glanced at her watch and then back out the window. It was getting late and she was anxious to get back to the lodge, but the prospect of warming up and drying out was tempting.

"Okay," she agreed, "but we can't stay long."

In no time Scott had the fire roaring. She watched as he filled the big kettle with water from a hand-operated pump and hung it on the hook over the fire. He really was a nice man. That would have meant a lot to her before... before she'd met Casey. Now she realized there was a world of difference between looking at a man and thinking he was nice and looking at a man and feeling a deep attraction to him. She'd never experienced those feelings before Casey, and she might never experience them again. In fact, she might regret being aware of their existence. One thing was certain, though: she would never again settle for those bland relationships she'd known in the past. Never again settle for "shared niceness" as the basis for love.

The flames crackled and popped and the icy air warmed. Scott uncovered a couch and pushed it over in front of the fire. He peeled off his coat and gloves and laid them on the stone hearth to dry. He sat down on the couch and began taking off his snow boots.

"C'mon," he insisted, "take your stuff off and dry out."

"We really don't have much time," Paige reminded him.

"We're fine," he said. "Now get over here in front of the fire."

Paige moved around to the front of the couch and stood. She peeled off her soggy gloves and laid them on the hearth.

Scott jumped up and eagerly tugged her coat off. He fussed over her like a mother hen, sitting her down on the couch and rubbing her cold hands between his.

Paige felt terribly ill at ease alone with this man, and she wished he'd stop hovering and leave her alone. She shivered involuntarily.

"You're still cold," he said, and headed for the sleeping loft. "I'll see if there's a blanket up here."

She didn't protest. At least the errand was giving her some breathing room.

He came back with a striped wool blanket and insisted on tucking it around her. He sat down close to her as he did so, and continued to arrange the blanket so that his arm ended up around her shoulders.

"We really need to get going Scott," she said nervously. "We're going to be late for the banquet."

"Relax," he said, giving her shoulders a little squeeze. "What do we wanna go to that old banquet for, anyway? We've got everything we could want right here. A big fire and food in the cupboards and plenty of booze."

"Scott..." she said, and leaned forward to stand up.

He pulled her back, and kissed her firmly on the lips.

"Scott," she said, irritated now by his behavior. "We don't..."

He pushed her down against the soft cushions of

the couch, pinning her body beneath his. She endured the kiss, not wanting to be too cruel with her rejection, preferring not to make her refusal a personal reflection on him, but instead to base it on the time factor.

"The plane," she said, when he gave her a breathing space. "I have to get back or I'll miss the plane."

"You're so beautiful," he breathed as though he hadn't heard her. "I want you all to myself. Please say you'll stay. Spend the night with me."

"No," she said, hating the situation more with each moment. "I can't. Really, I can't. My work...my job..."

He kissed her again long and hard, his tongue forcing its way between her stiff resisting lips, until she thought she would gag. Enough was enough. She struggled against him, doing all she could without actually trying to hurt him.

To her surprise and horror, struggling only seemed to excite him more. His breathing was ragged against her ear as he grabbed both her wrists and pinned them together above her head with one huge hand. With the other hand he roamed up and down her body, pawing, squeezing, tugging at her clothes. His urgent intimacy made her physically ill.

"Don't! Please!" Paige cried. "Stop it. Please stop it."

His searching fingers found the first button on her blouse and undid it.

"You're gonna love it," he whispered hoarsely. "You'll never settle for Cavanaugh after you've been with me."

Paige panicked. She knew it was useless to scream
or cry out. She was on her own, far from any hope of
rescue. She struggled in earnest now, with no thought
of whether she was hurting him or not. In fact, hurting him seemed the only possible hope.

The kettle whistled sharply and suddenly over the
fire. He drew back, startled, attention diverted. She
gathered all her strength and pushed. He was off balance just enough for the maneuver to work. He tumbled off the couch, striking his head on the sharp
corner of the hearth.

Paige scrambled over the back of the couch, landing on her hands and knees. By the time she gained
her feet he was standing in front of her, blood trick-
ling from a gash on his forehead.

She gasped at the sight of him. His face was twisted
with rage. He was an evil and dangerous stranger. The
shy, charming Scott Cannon was gone.

She backed slowly away from him, trying to keep
her wits, trying to reason with him.

"Scott, your head . . . it's bleeding. Let me look for
a bandage."

"You bitch," he said. "You stinking, rotten bitch.
Not gonna put out for me, huh. Think you can just
string me along. Think I'm not as good as Cavanaugh.
Well, you thought wrong. I'm gonna make you forget
Cavanaugh ever existed."

Paige kept backing up, hands to her mouth as
though stifling a silent scream. Hot tears coursed
freely down her cheeks, and she shook her head in a
slow-motion, horrified protest. She had never been so
frightened in her life.

He lunged for her, pinning her against the wall with his body. She fought him with everything she had, scratching, hitting and biting. But he seemed impervious to her. Again he grabbed her wrists and jerked her arms above her head, where he could pinion them with one hand. He ground his pelvis into her and ripped at her blouse with his free hand.

The sound of tearing cloth registered on the fringes of her mind, but she took no notice. She was in the grip of a blind, mindless fear. His head bent down toward her breasts and his body shifted, leaning out slightly to accommodate his bending head—leaning just enough to give her the room she needed to jerk her knee up hard and fast between his legs.

He doubled over, grunting and clutching at himself. Paige froze for an instant, horrified by the pain she'd inflicted. Then she bolted, grabbing a coat as she ran. She slammed through the door, stumbling in the drifted snow, running and stumbling again, not pausing for breath until she was well down the slope and could barely see the cabin through the trees.

Only then did she stop to put on the coat. It was Scott's coat. The thought repulsed her, but she pulled on the thick, puffy, down-filled nylon, anyway. It was huge on her, the cuffs hanging well past her hands and the waist halfway to her knees. The sudden picture of Scott having to wear her size-ten coat back to the lodge made her laugh hysterically, sinking to the ground with weak and trembling legs. The laughter turned gradually to tears and finally disintegrated into sobs. She felt immense relief, laced with a strong dose of anger and disgust.

She drew in a deep cleansing breath and gathered her strength. She picked herself up and studied the terrain. There was a fairly well-marked trail to the lodge. They'd been on it when the snowmobile had stopped. If she could just make her way back to the snowmobile as a starting point she felt certain she could follow that trail to the lodge on foot.

What if Scott tried to come after her? The thought sent her into a panic, and she dashed farther into the trees, before she got a hold of herself. She leaned against the rough-barked trunk of a tall pine and labored to catch her breath. There was no room for panic here. The mountains and the cold would be far more dangerous than Scott Cannon if she got lost. She had to keep her wits and get control of the situation.

Carefully she considered the position of the cabin, the position of the lowering sun and the landscape around her. When she finally found the snowmobile she felt like shouting for joy. Nothing would stop her now. She had found the trail by herself and she would find the lodge, too.

She walked briskly, swinging her arms, watching for spots where she might stumble or fall. She had escaped and she was on the homestretch, and everything was all right. She relaxed the tight grip she'd had on her thoughts and let them wander freely.

Why? Why had this happened to her?

Her mind played over the sequence of events. Scott had been charming. She hadn't imagined that. There'd been nothing in his behavior to forewarn her. She'd always considered herself such a good judge of masculine character. In fact, that was the major reason she dated so little—she evaluated and cataloged men quickly enough to eliminate most of them before she had wasted much of her time dating the unacceptable ones. What had gone wrong? Had her judgment grown faulty? How could she have seen a complete lunatic as charming and shy?

Had she done something in particular to set him off? No, she didn't think so, but wait . . . what had that business been about Casey? She'd been too frightened at the time to listen very clearly, but it had been something about making her forget Casey or being better than Casey, and then something about her thinking Scott wasn't as good as Casey.

What could Scott Cannon possibly know of how she felt about Casey? Unless he'd heard it from Casey. Unless Casey had told Scott the intimate details of last night. The thought sickened her, but it made perfect sense. Scott knew everything, and he had turned it into a contest. He was trying to "win out" over Casey. He apparently thought so highly of his sexual techniques that he believed one round of lovemaking with him, even if it had to be forced on her, would make her instantly forget Casey, thereby making Scott the victor. The entire situation was disgusting.

Did Casey know of Scott's intentions? She thought back to the look he'd given her when he saw her with Scott. Had the hurt and disappointment she'd seen in his eyes been caused only by the thought that he might be losing to Scott? And if that was true, weren't both men equally to blame?

She wished she could have them both thrown in jail! But what would she accuse Casey of? Knowing what was going on? That was hardly a crime. And even Scott. What could she prove? What would it look like to all the people who had seen her being friendly with him at the lodge and then voluntarily leaving with him on the snowmobile? He was a dangerous animal, but she'd never be able to prove it.

She shivered and hugged herself as she walked. Her feet were as heavy and leaden as concrete blocks. Her hands burned with cold inside the hanging sleeves, and her face felt completely numb.

Suddenly the full implications of Casey's knowing hit her. If all she had been was the object of a contest between him and Scott, if that was the only reason he had continued to pursue her... then he truly was the despicable person she had at first believed him to be. The thought was surprisingly painful.

She had begun to hope—to hope what? That he really was a good person. That he was a decent man in spite of the fact that he'd followed her to her room like a tomcat after a female in heat that first day, when she'd mistaken him for a bellman. A decent man, in spite of the fact that he admitted "expecting" strange women to proposition him. A decent man, in spite of the fact that he'd taken her to her room and made love to her the night before when she'd had so much wine she was not responsible for her actions. Maybe the blame was not all his, but still it added to the picture as a whole. That he was a decent man in spite of his arrogance and his conceit and his self-centered manipulation of the people around him.

What a fool she was! What a stupid fool! The man

was obviously detestable. She had to be simple-minded to have felt an attraction to a man like that. Her original assessment had been correct. Her judgment was still intact.

The sound of an engine cut sharply into her thoughts. The snowmobile! Scott was after her! She turned and ran blindly into the trees. Hide, hide. She had to find a place to hide. Frantically she darted this way and that, searching for something to get behind. The log—the fallen log was big enough. She dove behind it, clawing at the snow with her bare hands, trying to dig out a space for herself.

She curled up in a ball, arms over her head, and tried to steady her breathing. He wouldn't find her. As long as she didn't move she was safe. She crouched there for several minutes, until the droning sound was almost out of range, before she realized that the machine had been coming from the wrong direction. It couldn't have been Scott. And besides, Scott's snowmobile was inoperative. Or was it? Had that been only a ploy? A way to get her to the cabin alone?

Wearily she stood and brushed snow off her clothes. Her panic had just cost her a chance at a ride back. She could have flagged the person down. She could have asked for help. If only she'd have been thinking more clearly.

Around her the shadows were lengthening. Dusk settled on the forest, bringing with it an eerie gray silence. She could no longer see very far in any direction. It would be dark before long. A person could lose the path in the dark. A person could freeze to death, lost in the dark.

Fright clutched at her chest and she ran, angling

back toward the path, zigzagging in a clumsy lope. The sound of cracking ice and the sensation of falling hit her together. She flayed her arms, reaching out, grabbing at the air, but there was no help. With a gentle whoosh the icy water sucked her down, shocking her body into a frozen immobility. Her tortured lungs gasped for a breath as she sank.

And then her feet were touching, her bottom touching. She was sitting on rocks. It was shallow! She could make it out without even swimming. She willed her body to respond. Willed it to move, to crawl, to drag itself up out of the frozen spring.

Snow. She was back on land. She was okay. She tried to stand, to walk, but she kept falling. She felt numb, groggy, unable to focus. The path. She had to make it back to the path. Had to keep going. Make it to the lodge.

It had taken Casey a while to figure out Scott Cannon's plan. First he had tracked down the owner of the snowmobile, who had mentioned in conversation how funny Scott had been about wanting to know things about the machine's engine. Like, for example, what could go wrong with it.

Armed with that information Casey had immediately thought of the cabin. It belonged to the lodge and he'd been to parties there. More important, he knew of several instances when Scott had used it to "entertain" ladies back in the days before the violent Cannon divorce scene... back in the days when Scott still had a wife in his room at the lodge to hide from.

Of course, there was no wife in Scott's room now.

No Mrs. Cannon at all. So why the cabin routine? Why go to all that trouble? Why not just take Paige up to his empty room in the lodge? There was certainly no one to object.

Unless it was Paige. Unless Scott had been worried that Paige wouldn't go willingly to his room. Unless he wanted her in that secluded cabin so there would be no one to hear her objections.

Casey felt a cold stab of fear in his gut. Scott Cannon was no good. He'd never been any good. And now that his wife had walked out, he was positively unbalanced. Not the kind of man for a woman to be alone with in a mountain cabin.

Scott would be furious at him for showing up, ruining the little "stranded together in a cabin" scene. What about Paige? How would she feel? Would she look on him as a rescuer or an intruder? Would she be grateful to him, or would she be angry at him?

He didn't know the answers, but he had to go just the same. He couldn't leave her out there with Cannon if there was any chance she didn't want to be there.

He pulled his coat collar closer, shoved a heavy-duty flashlight into his pocket and mounted the snowmobile.

"Don't be too long," the man called to him as he skimmed away. "It's about dark."

The trail to the cabin was well used and easy to follow. He flew across the dusk-shrouded landscape at top speed, heedless of the cold, whipping wind against his face.

She was up there somewhere with Scott Cannon.

He had to admit he was jealous as hell, but it was so much more than that. Scott Cannon hated him... hated him enough to try using an innocent woman like Paige to hurt him, not caring that he would be hurting Paige in the process.

The more Casey thought about it, the more convinced he was that he had discovered the motive for Scott's actions. He'd made no secret of his feelings for Paige. Scott could have learned of them through numerous sources. And to Scott's twisted mind it had probably looked like the perfect opportunity for revenge.

He could see the cabin now, a dark shape among the trees. The windows glowed with firelight. He roared right up to the door and stepped in without knocking.

The scene was a peaceful one. Firelight danced on the walls, and Scott was stretched out on a couch with a drink in his hand.

"Where is she?" Casey demanded, his voice heavy with threat.

"You're too late this time," Scott said, taking a long drink of what looked like whiskey. "She's gone."

"What do you mean 'gone'? I saw the snowmobile down the hill where you 'fixed' it not to run. How can she be gone? How'd she leave?"

"Burns you up, huh?" Scott said, standing and taking another drink. He moved around to the back of the couch, where he could face Casey squarely, his expression contorted with hate. "No Cavanaugh to the rescue again, huh? Like with my wife."

"Where is she, Cannon?"

"I told you. She's gone. You missed out on this

one." He swirled the liquid in his glass with a smirk and turned back toward the couch. "And a damned tender little morsel, too," he added with a snicker.

A dam of rage broke within Casey. He grabbed Scott's shoulder and spun him around. Roughly he took hold of the front of Scott's shirt. "Where is she?" he shouted.

Scott laughed, and the cabin was filled with the evil echoing sound.

Something snapped. All control was lost. There was the sound of the whiskey glass breaking, and then the cabin was filled with the sickening sounds of flesh striking flesh, bones cracking against stone and wood, animallike grunts of pain.

When thought finally returned to Casey he was standing over a slumped and groaning Scott. He reached up to touch the aching spot on the back of his head, and his hand came away bloody. He could feel his left eye swelling rapidly. He knelt down beside Scott and shook him roughly.

"Where is she?" he repeated between clenched teeth.

"She left... walking... walking back to the lodge," Scott said with a grimace of pain. "Damned frigid bitch... little snow won't hurt her."

Casey leaped to his feet and flew through the door. She was out there somewhere, alone and cold and possibly lost. He had to find her—fast.

His mind raced as he sped down the hill. He could go right back to the lodge and call for a search patrol, but that would waste so much time, and every minute could be important at this point.

She was smart. She would have realized the trail

led straight back to the lodge. And he had no doubt she would have found the trail. Then why hadn't he seen her on his way up? Had she already been down, unconscious, maybe—and he'd sped right by her? Could he have missed seeing her?

He continued a short distance at top speed, confident that she had managed to travel awhile before she...before she what? Slipped and hit her head, or twisted her ankle? Fell into a snow-covered crevice? Or simply passed out from the cold? The possibilities for danger, especially for an inexperienced person without the proper clothing, were endless.

He traveled slowly now, shining his high-powered flashlight in an arc from right to left through the trees and across the ground. The snow sparkled brilliantly in the beam of light. He stopped periodically and shut off the engine to listen and call out her name. His calls echoed back to him in the icy silence.

Time ceased to exist for him. He had to look at his watch to determine whether minutes or hours had passed.

And through it all his mind kept repeating the same phrase, *let her be all right... let her be all right,* over and over, sometimes demanding, sometimes angry, sometimes pleading.

He was three-quarters of the way to the lodge, when he found her. The sweeping beam of light revealed her prone form beside the trail. He slammed the controls of his machine to Off and ran to her.

"Paige! Paige!" he cried, kneeling in the snow and gathering her in his arms.

She was limp and lifeless. Her clothes were cold

and wet and crusted with snow and ice. He pulled off a glove and touched her cheeks with his fingers. There was no warmth to her skin at all. Frantically he felt her wrists and neck for a pulse, but he could find nothing.

In despair, he clutched her to his chest and held her, gently rocking back and forth in the snow. He cradled her head in the bend of his arm and bent to touch his cheek against hers. Her cap fell off, and he squeezed his eyes shut in agony as her long hair spilled out against his face.

It was then that he heard the sound. Such a tiny sound he might have missed it, had his ear not been so close. A minute rush of air, an infinitesimal moan. A sign of life.

His heart leaped and adreneline sped into his veins. He grabbed her roughly, shaking her and coaxing her. He jerked off her sodden, oversized jacket and wrapped her in his own. He rubbed her hands and face and slapped her sharply on the cheek.

She moaned again and moved slightly.

He worked his gloves onto her stiff hands and wrapped his long wool scarf around her head and neck.

"It's okay," he said over and over. "Casey's here. Everything's okay."

It was awkward to hold her limp body while riding the snowmobile, but he was too determined to fail. Slowly he traversed the distance to the lodge, clasping her tightly and repeating reassuring phrases as he went. The icy wind cut through the cloth of his shirt and burned his bare hands and neck to numbness. He gritted his teeth and willed himself not to shiver or weaken.

He pulled directly up to the front steps of the lodge. Slowly, carefully, he carried her inside. His muscles quivered from cold and exhaustion. Her limp body grew heavier and heavier in his arms.

Several lodge employees rushed up to him, all talking at once. "What is it... what's wrong... what happened... is she hurt?"

"A doctor," he said. "A bed... blankets." He clenched his jaw muscles to keep his teeth from chattering.

Quickly they arranged a room and tucked her into a bed. Casey sank into a chair and watched as the lodge people scurried around, turning up the room heat and piling more blankets on Paige's still form.

Someone draped a blanket around his shoulders, and Casey accepted it gratefully. He drew it close around his shoulders like a cape and finally allowed himself to shiver inside the safe, warm folds of wool. Someone handed him a cup of steaming coffee, and he held it with numb, clumsy fingers and stared at Paige's waxen face.

The doctor arrived, wearing ski clothes and carrying a brightly colored tote bag. She bent over Paige a moment in silence, then spoke as she fished in her bag.

"Who brought her in?" she asked briskly.

"I did," Casey answered.

"Has she had a fall or some other injury... besides the exposure?"

"I don't know. I found out she was walking to the lodge and went looking for her. Found her like that. Judging from the distance she'd covered, she couldn't have been unconscious for more than thirty minutes."

There was silence in the room as the doctor worked. She listened to Paige's heart, checked her blood pressure and lifted her unresponsive eyelids to check her pupils.

"Will she be all right?" Casey asked.

"Good as new," the doctor said, pulling a syringe and vial from her bag. Deftly she popped the plastic cap off the disposible needle and filled the syringe with the contents of the vial.

"What's that?" Casey asked anxiously.

"Atrophine," the doctor answered, and swabbed a spot on Paige's upper arm with a cotton ball. "To speed up her heart a little, get that blood circulating," she explained as she plunged the needle expertly into the exposed flesh.

"She may be out for a while," the doctor said as she tucked the blankets back around Paige's chin. "If you get a chance, try to get some hot broth down her. Call me tonight if any problems arise. Otherwise I'll check on her in the morning." She gathered up her instruments and turned toward Casey. "She's lucky you found her."

"Wish I'd have gotten there sooner," he said.

"Now what about you?"

"What?" he asked, bewildered as to her meaning.

"Take off your shirt and let me look."

"No, I'm not going to take off my shirt. I'm not the patient here."

"Well, you certainly could be," she said shortly. "Is there anything else besides your face?"

"What about my face?"

"You need some stitches in the corner of your eye for starters," she said, pulling antiseptic and syringe and stitch kit from her bag. "Who knows what's underneath all that dried blood. I suppose you ran into a few large trees or stray fists or something while you were out hunting for her tonight?"

"I'm fine," Casey insisted.

She acted as though she hadn't heard, and began giving directions to people in the room.

"Now just wait a minute," Casey protested, shifting and spilling hot coffee on his leg.

She ignored him. Someone reached out and took the cup from his hands, while someone else moved a floor lamp over to provide better light. The doctor pushed his head back against the chair and roughly scrubbed at his face. He hadn't realized how many raw, sore spots he had. Scott must have landed some good ones.

She took four tiny stitches, telling him that the scar would look just like a smile line, though he himself voiced no concern. The thought of a scar didn't bother him. The thought of that needle going in and out of his skin did. He squeezed his eyes shut and clenched his jaw, and tried to take his mind off the process by thinking of all the good bulls he'd ridden that year.

"Needle phobia, huh?" the doctor said, smiling for the first time.

He glared at her. It was hard to be tough all the time. Bulls he could handle but needles were another story.

She picked up her bag and stood looking down at him. "Get some rest," she said. "There's nothing more you can do tonight." She handed him a packet.

"Take two of these every four hours. I know you aren't in any pain now, but you're still half-frozen. When you get warmed up your face will start throbbing and that goose egg on your head will ache."

Casey watched her leave the room. He spoke briefly with the remaining lodge people and insisted on sitting with Paige for the night, promising to call down for broth if she woke. As soon as they left the room, he turned off all the lights but one, dropped the pills in the trash and pulled his chair over close to the head of Paige's bed.

She looked better already. He reached out, touching her forehead and then her cheek. The warmth of her skin was reassuring. She was going to be fine— good as new, the doctor had said.

He settled into the chair and studied her face. How would she feel when she woke? Would she be glad to see him, or indifferent or—his jaw tightened at the thought of it—would she hate him? Would she realize that Scott had been using her against him and hold him responsible?

Her sleeping face gave no answers. If she did blame him everything would be over. He could never undo so much damage. She would never forgive him. He would have to live with that and give up all hope.

## Chapter Six

Paige awoke in a confused fog. The dimly lit room wasn't familiar. The haggard, swollen face staring down at her wasn't familiar.

She heard someone on the phone asking for broth to be sent. She tried to sit up, but she was imprisoned in a tight cocoon of blankets.

"Paige," a man's voice said.

"Where am I?"

"At the lodge. In a room at the lodge."

"Did I miss the plane?"

"Yes," he said gently, "but don't worry, there's one tomorrow."

The incident in the cabin suddenly came back to her.

"Scott," she said. "Don't let Scott in!"

"I won't," the voice answered soothingly.

"Or Casey," she mumbled, her eyelids growing heavy again. "His fault, too...whole thing...both their faults." She vaguely heard the broth being delivered, and she managed to take a few sips, before she slipped back into a deep sleep.

"I can't believe it! Is everything I heard true? The one year I stay here in Denver and it turns out to be the most action-packed ski trip in history!" Judy exclaimed as she shut the door to Paige's room and cleared off a chair for herself. "I rushed up as soon as I heard you were back. Are you all right? Do you need me to get anything for you?"

Paige sank wearily to the bed, pulling pillows into place so she could comfortably lean back against the headboard in a sitting position. "I'm fine," she said, "just tired. I'm glad to be going home. I can't wait to get away from all this...and I miss Trisha. I want to see Trisha."

Judy eyed her strangely.

"What's wrong?" Paige asked. "Do you think I'm running away?"

"No, it's not that. I just hadn't realized how involved you were in your work with the child."

"What's that supposed to mean? Do I detect a hint of disapproval in your voice? Just the other night I remember you bragging about what I do with Trisha. Have you suddenly changed your mind?"

"No," Judy said quietly. "It's just...well, you sounded so emotionally tied to her just then."

"What's wrong with that?"

"Nothing's wrong with it. But do they recommend that type of thing in the program? It seems like such an invitation to be hurt. After all, she has a life of her own. She's not yours. She's not even related to you. She could disappear from your world on a moment's notice."

"What do you mean?" Paige asked.

Judy shrugged. "Her parents could take her out of the program."

"Her father took off. She only has a mother."

"Okay, her mother could take her out of the program."

"Her mother wouldn't do that. She knows how much I mean to Trisha," Paige insisted.

"Oh, come on, Paige. People's lives change. The mother could marry a rock musician and go on the road, or get a job offer from the White House. People's lives change, and even though the mother might not want to take Trisha out of the program, her circumstances could force her to. If you aren't aware of that and if you aren't at least subconsciously prepared for it, you're setting yourself up for a helluva heartbreak. Also...it makes me wonder if that little girl isn't some kind of substitute in your life for an adult relationship."

"I don't know...I just can't think straight right now," Paige said wearily.

"All right," Judy said. "Then explain to me how in the world you got mixed up with Scott Cannon?"

Paige sighed. "Pure stupidity, I guess."

"Well, please, fill me in," Judy urged. "There are just a whole lot of things I don't understand about all this."

Paige began by outlining how she had met Scott, her initial impressions of Scott and how taken in she'd been by his shy, charming act.

"You and about a million other women," Judy said. "He does his country-boy routine and the women drop like flies. Don't get me wrong...he's not the only cowboy playing games with women—his act is just one of the best. Academy Award material. I guess I should have warned you about him ahead of time, but I just never dreamed that you...well, that *you* could be fooled by any of that."

"I know, I know. Practical, sensible, clearheaded Paige. Who'd have ever thought? The trouble is, I haven't been practical or sensible or clearheaded the past few days. I've been so confused about Casey... I...I just can't seem to think straight."

"You're right on the nose about that," Judy agreed. "You haven't been thinking straight about Casey at all."

"What do you mean by that?"

"I mean that you've had yourself convinced Casey is some sort of villain, and he's not. He's one terrific guy, and he's genuinely interested in you. Maybe if you hadn't been so busy casting Casey as the bad guy you'd have seen that Scott was the one to beware of."

"Let me tell you about your terrific guy!" Paige retorted angrily. "Everything that happened was his fault!"

"What are you talking about?" Judy asked incredulously.

"I'm talking about he and Scott Cannon having some kind of contest going. I'm talking about Casey taking advantage of me when I had all that wine the other night and boasting about it to Scott, and Scott accepting it as a challenge and trying to make the same 'score,' with big hopes that he might even best Casey and have me praising his prowess over Casey's. Some terrific guy, huh?''

"No," Judy said, shaking her head. "It isn't true. Casey would never be involved in anything like that."

"Oh? And why else would Scott be so determined and keep mumbling about getting even with Casey and being better than Casey. And why would my refusal send him into such a rage, yelling about me not thinking he was as good as Casey. Unless he knew about Casey's 'success' with me the other night. It all adds up."

Judy thought for a moment in silence. "Casey didn't take advantage of you the other night," she began hesitantly. "I know...I, well I wasn't going to say anything because I figured it was pretty embarrassing for you...but I came by your room. Ken and I decided we were too full and too tired to do any dancing, so we went back to the hotel. I went up to your room to check on you. Casey was just leaving. He was glad to see me. Said you needed more help getting ready for bed and he wasn't about to be the one to do it. Said if he did, you'd just be furious at him in the morning.

"I went on in, and you were so out of it you still thought I was Casey. You were wanting him to take off the rest of your clothes and...well, if Casey had wanted to make love to you, believe me, you'd have had no objections. Seemed to me you were the one trying to take advantage."

Paige felt her cheeks flame, and she stared down at her hands in silence. She knew deep down that Judy was telling the truth, and she suspected she'd known it all along.

"Casey would never have breathed your name to Scott, much less bragged to him about you," Judy said. "But I think I see what happened." She tapped her chin with her index finger a moment. "You fell right into the middle of the Cannon-Cavanaugh feud thing. You see, Scott hates Casey. They had quite a run-in over Scott's wife."

"Over his wife?" Paige asked weakly, imagining all sorts of horrible scenarios.

"Not the way you think. There was nothing between Casey and her. Just passing friends, the way she was with all the other cowboys. She never looked at anybody but Scott. Acted like she was crazy about the creep."

Judy took a deep breath and leaned back in her chair. "Scott's wife was a really beautiful girl. Worked as a model before she married him. He got quite a charge out of parading her around at parties and stuff and having all the attention focused on 'his woman.' But he just couldn't seem to settle down and be a husband. He played around as much after the wedding as he had before. Then he got to humiliating her in public, and, well, Lord knows why she stayed as long as she did.

"About six months ago a bunch of the guys were all sitting down in a hotel coffee shop, when Scott's wife ran in. She wanted somebody to drive her to the airport, fast. Before anyone could volunteer, Scott

came runnin' in after her. Slapped her in front of all
those guys and started dragging her out of there.
Casey stood up and said, 'Wait a minute, don't treat
her like that.' Scott yelled at him to mind his own
business and just kept yanking his wife along, with
her crying and fighting him and getting banged
around pretty bad.

"Finally Casey stepped in and made Scott let her
go. She said a few choice words to Scott in front of all
of his friends. Told him that if he were a man like
Casey, instead of an animal, maybe he'd be able to
keep a wife.

"Then Casey not only drove her to the airport, he
loaded her up in his own plane and flew her wherever
she wanted to go. She filed for divorce shortly there-
after.

"No one thought the divorce would have any effect
on Scott, but it did. I don't think it was losing his wife
so much that bothered him as the fact that everyone
knew about it. He saw it as a public humiliation. A
major defeat in his life.

"Scott's hated Casey ever since. He twisted it around
in his mind to where everything that happened was
Casey's fault. Once when he was drinking he even
accused Casey of 'taking his wife away from him.' Talk
about ridiculous!

"All that hate had probably just about reached the
boiling point. And—" Judy shrugged. "Well, Casey's
obvious interest in you was big news on the grape-
vine—he so seldom shows any real interest in any particular woman—and when Scott heard about it he
must have seen you as a means toward revenge."

Paige was silent, digesting everything she'd heard.

"And you don't think Casey came out to the cabin just to see if Scott had been successful?" she finally asked.

"No! He went looking for you because he knows what a rat Scott is, and he was worried about you. If you'd seen Scott before he left you'd know he and Casey weren't just comparing notes in that cabin."

Paige raised her eyebrows in question.

"You didn't hear what a terrible run-in they had?"

Paige shook her head.

"It was so strange. I've never heard of Casey being involved in any kind of violence, but I guess all of us have our limits and Scott pushed Casey over his with his treatment of you. Anyway, I don't know the exact tally of injuries, but he had a cast on one hand and a big bandage on the side of his head, and someone said it would be at least four months till he could even think about roping."

"You're kidding!"

"No. Course, Casey didn't look too great himself," Judy added ruefully. "But, then, I forget. You saw him last night."

"I didn't," Paige said. "I haven't seen him at all."

"But he told me he didn't leave your room until you woke up and talked to him," Judy said.

"Oh, God! Was that him?" Paige said, remembering vaguely a swollen, haggard specter over her bed.

She buried her face in her hands and thought it all out. It fit. All the facts Judy had just given her fit. She had misjudged Casey badly.

"I can't believe it," Paige said. "I can't believe he went out there to save me and went through all that and I... I thought he was... I've got to see him," she said, jumping off the bed. "I've got to see him. To thank him. To tell him..." Her voice trailed off as she caught Judy's expression.

"You're too late. He's gone already," Judy said sadly. "He was so down. He said it was his fault that Scott used you for revenge. He said the best thing he could do for you now was to get out of your life. And he thought you'd be glad to get back home and never see him or another rodeo again."

Paige swallowed hard, but she was unable to stop the hot tears from flowing down her cheeks. "What do I do now?" she asked, her voice choked and pathetic.

"Only you can decide that," Judy said softly. "It's all up to you. You can go home to California and forget all this ever happened, or you can figure out a way to see Casey again. It's as simple as that."

"And if I do see him again, what would I say? How could I make up for everything I've thought...for the way I've treated him?"

"If you do see him again," Judy said carefully, "just let things take their course. Don't worry in advance and prepare speeches. Play it by ear, as Casey would say, just play it by ear."

As Paige packed her belongings a myriad of questions plagued her. She zipped her hang-up bag. Should she see Casey again? She latched her suitcase. Should she go home and forget about him? She buckled her carryon. What would happen if she saw him again? She snapped her typewriter case shut. Could she forget about him? She gathered up her notebooks and papers. Did she want to forget about him?

Riding to the airport and boarding the plane gave her a brief rest, but once safely seated and buckled in, the questions returned. For the first time in her life she had no definite answers. There was no black or white here. No right or wrong. She felt lost and confused.

She stared out the plane's oval window and watched the Denver landscape miniaturize and then fade into nothing. She felt both relief and sadness at leaving. She would have many memories of the time spent in Colorado. It was almost as if she had passed some kind of milestone here, and her life would never be quite the same because of it. And, she thought with a brief inward smile, she could tell Trisha that she had seen an eagle soar.

Once back to her office she discovered that her career expectations had changed, too. What she had seen as the familiar safety of her desk looked boring and restrictive now. The assignment she had dreaded and seen as hopeless now seemed like her big chance.

She tried to explain it to Trisha, but the twelve-year-old just looked at her as though she'd recited a story with an unintelligible punch line. Immediately Paige felt guilty. She was the one who was supposed to be supplying the strength and wisdom. What had she expected? Advice? Understanding? From a child?

She turned her work in with shaking hands and paced for hours waiting for the verdict. She wanted it to be a success. She wanted to do other things just like it. She wanted to reach out and touch the world, not hide at her desk anymore.

She held her breath when Miss Carson appeared at the door. Paige watched the woman enter and walk to the window. For a moment she did nothing but stare out across the sky. Then she turned to face Paige.

"I've always believed you had more to offer, Paige," she said. "I knew you didn't want to go on any further, but I firmly believed that you had a talent you weren't using. I believed that you could join the big leagues . . . that you'd be good." The woman paused and drew in a deep breath. "I was wrong."

Paige's heart sunk.

"I was wrong," Maggie Carson repeated. "You're not good . . ." She grinned. "You're terrific! You're absolutely wonderful!"

Paige leaped from her chair and hugged the older woman tightly. It was settled. There was no turning back.

Her Saturday with Trisha became a celebration. They ate pizza and ice cream until they thought they would burst, and then they went back to Paige's apartment to play Pente and drink hot cider.

"You know that trip to Denver?" Trisha began. Paige had answered endless questions about the trip, and they had all begun with the same sentence.

"Yes," Paige said.

"My mom was asking me some stuff."

"What kind of stuff?" Paige said.

Trisha moved her Pente bead. "Stuff like if you went to see a man."

"What did you tell her?" Paige asked evenly.

"I said no. You were just working. You never do nothin' with men, and she said it figured."

Paige made her move and waited.

"Is that right?" Trisha said.

"Never do anything," Paige corrected.

The girl grimaced and restated her question with childish persistence. "All right, is it true about you never do anything with men?"

"The part about me going to Denver to work is right," Paige said.

"How 'bout the other stuff? About you never doin' nothin' with men?"

"Well, I do have dates once in a while," Paige answered.

"Good," Trisha said with relief. "I'm gonna tell my mom you have dates. She said you were so uptight no man would want you." The girl smiled. "I knew that wasn't true," she said.

Paige felt a little sliver of hurt dart through her chest. The comments were those of a child. There was no reason they should hurt her—but they did. She wanted to shout to Trisha that a man had wanted her. *Tell your nosy mother that.* An exciting, wonderful man had wanted her. But then what? Would she then admit she'd botched things so badly that she'd probably destroyed whatever feelings he had for her?

Her career future was settled now, and he became the major question in her life. It ate at her day and night, lurking on the fringes of her mind, never far from her thoughts. She would glance at her watch and realize suddenly she'd been thinking about him, she'd been wondering.

She tried to convince herself she didn't want to see him; she never wanted to see him again. She tried to recreate her feelings of anger and disgust toward him by remembering all the incidents—the bellboy mix-up, the press party, the dinner. But somehow, knowing all she knew now, understanding all she did now, she could forgive his actions, even if she didn't condone them. And it was hard to find fault with the fact that he had gone out after her and saved her life.

So instead of convincing herself she never wanted to see him again, all her efforts, all of her thinking only made her realize that she had been badly mistaken about him all along, that she wanted to see him more than ever.

She tried to immerse herself in her work, to forget about him, but it was impossible. Like a specter, the question loomed over her life. Should she see him? And gradually, ever so gradually, the question changed from should she see him, to how could she see him? How could she see him without it being embarrassing or strained or so tense that neither of them could behave normally?

How could she arrange to see him without turning it into either a confrontation or an act of submission? Most important, how could she ask him to meet her without admitting to him that she wanted to see him, without giving away her own feelings before she had some sense of his?

The answer was slow in coming to her, but when it came it was so perfect, so totally beautiful, that she marveled at her own cleverness. She had often observed but never experienced the good-natured scheming and planning that had gone into boy-girl relationships in high school and college. She had to admit that the anticipation and the wonderful devi-

# First Class Romance

Delivered to your door by

## Silhouette Special Edition®

(See inside for special 4 FREE book offer)

# Find romance at your door with 4 FREE novels from Silhouette Special Edition!

Slip away to a world that's only as far away as your mailbox. A world of romance, where the pace of life is as gentle as a kiss, and as fast as the pounding of a lover's heartbeat. Wrap yourself in the special pleasure of having Silhouette Special Edition novels arrive at your home.

By filling out and mailing the attached postage-paid order card you'll receive FREE 4 new Silhouette Special Edition romances and a Cameo Tote Bag (a $16.99 value).

You'll also receive an extra bonus: our monthly Silhouette Books Newsletter. Then approximately every 4 weeks we'll send you six more Silhouette Special Edition romances to examine FREE for 15 days. If you decide to keep them, you'll pay just $11.70 (a $15.00 value) with no extra charge for home delivery and at no risk! You'll have the option to cancel at any time. Just drop us a note. Your first 4 books and the Tote Bag are yours to keep in any case.

*Silhouette Special Edition*®

# EXTRA BONUS
## *A Free Cameo Tote*

You'll receive brand-new
novels as they're published!

FILL OUT THIS POSTPAID CARD AND MAIL TODAY!

NO POSTAGE
NECESSARY
IF MAILED
IN THE
UNITED STATES

## BUSINESS REPLY CARD
FIRST CLASS   PERMIT NO. 194   CLIFTON, N.J.

*Postage will be paid by addressee*

**Silhouette Books
120 Brighton Road
P.O. BOX 5084
Clifton, NJ 07015-9956**

# Mail this card today for your
# 4 FREE BOOKS
## and this Tote Bag
## (a $16.99 value)!

FILL OUT THIS POSTCARD AND MAIL TODAY!

ousness of it was fun. She caught herself chuckling over it all at the oddest times.

Later that week, after the Denver material had been submitted to the clients for approval, Paige was called to the conference table for an afternoon meeting. She was handed a cup of tea and given the good news that the clients had loved her work and were clamoring for more of the same. They had sent a representative to discuss future possibilities.

"Did you have any particular rodeo in mind, Mr. Baker?" Paige asked him.

"San Antonio seems like an interesting choice," he answered quickly. "And it's quite soon on the rodeo schedule."

Paige agreed that that sounded fine.

A few ideas were presented for the focus of the piece. Paige sat back in silence and listened. Mr. Baker did not seem overly impressed with any of them. Good.

When the time seemed right she leaned forward and cleared her throat. Ten pairs of eyes fastened on her. The palms of her hands felt damp and there was a knot in the pit of her stomach.

"What about concentrating on a major personality?" she said. "Taking an in-depth look at the person's activities and life during the entire week of the rodeo, not just the period of time they perform?"

Baker screwed up his forehead in thought. "It could work," he said. "But so much would depend on who the personality was. He has to be someone who's a real standout. Someone with a lot of public appeal. And someone with pretty good character... after all, we want to keep this positive and upbeat...and we don't want to spotlight someone who's been used a great deal and overexposed.''

Paige swallowed hard and tried to speak nonchalantly. "I was thinking of Casey Cavanaugh," she said.

Baker's eyes widened. Then he shook his head and laughed. "Great idea," he said. "But apparently you haven't been around rodeo enough to know. He doesn't cooperate with the press, and what you're suggesting would require full cooperation to work."

"I'm aware of Mr. Cavanaugh's eccentricities," Paige assured him. "But I think there's a chance he might agree to our proposal. I'd like to give it a try."

"By all means, Miss Bannister. If you think there's a chance, then go for it. And you know," he said with his whole body generating excitement, "if you can pull this off, we'll be prepared to add significant financial strength to this entire campaign."

Her plan was in gear. Now came the most crucial step—Casey's agreement.

Back at her desk, Paige spent an hour inventing reasons not to pick up the phone. She had wasted a great deal of time tracking down his unlisted number. She had sharpened her pencils and brewed herself a fresh cup of tea. There were no excuses left, no more reasons to keep from lifting that receiver and dialing. She had been warned by her last contact that Casey wasn't home much, and if she didn't reach him today her chances of catching him before San Antonio were slim.

She drew in a deep breath and dialed the number with shaking fingers.

"Hello."

The sound of his voice made her heart skip a beat.

"Hello, Casey...this is Paige Bannister."

Silence. Had he hung up? She held her breath, expecting the buzz of the dial tone any moment.

"I...I looked for you in Denver, but you'd already gone," she said finally.

"Yeah," he said. "Leaving seemed the best move at that point."

"I didn't get a chance to thank you for bringing me in. I guess you saved my life...I'm very grateful."

He said nothing, but she could tell he was listening.

"Are you going to San Antonio?" he asked.

"Yes."

"I'll be there, too," she said hesitantly. "For my firm...working. I thought...well, I was wondering if..." She could feel him waiting on the other end of the line. "If you might let me feature you for this piece I'm doing."

There, she'd said it. She gripped the receiver so tightly her knuckles turned white. If he was still interested he'd say yes. If he was still attracted to her he'd say yes. If there was still a chance for anything at all between them he'd say yes. In just a tiny fraction of time she would know, one way or the other.

"So this is strictly a business call, huh?" His voice sounded harder now. "You ought to know I don't do interviews."

"This wouldn't be a formal interview situation," she said quickly. "It would be more like a week in the life of Casey Cavanaugh. I'd just follow you around while you went about your normal activities. And remember, I'm not working for a publication, I'm actually working for professional rodeo. Our firm was hired by PRCA sponsors to promote the sport as a whole. The piece will be very positive. I'm sure there won't be anything you'd object to in it."

Time crawled while she waited for his answer.

"And what if I say no?" he asked.

"The sponsors may tell me to ask another cowboy," she said evenly. "Or they may tell me not to go to San Antonio at all."

She squeezed her eyes tightly shut and crossed her fingers. If only she had ESP. If only she could will him to say yes.

"All right," he said slowly. "But on one condition. Everything is on my terms. Everything. I say what, when, where, why and how. And I get final approval of the copy."

Paige agreed quickly. She could barely contain her excitement long enough to finish the call. As soon as she hung up she jumped from her chair, filled with delight and excitement.

He wanted to see her. He wanted to see her badly enough to put aside his no-press rule. She felt as giddy and lighthearted as a schoolgirl.

She paced around the office till five o'clock came. Then she went home and paced around her apartment. She was too nervous to eat, too keyed up to read and too agitated to sit still and watch television. She wondered how she would ever get through the week.

She spent the days remembering him. The deep blue of his eyes. The chiseled line of his jaw. The tiny scar at his temple—were there other scars now from his fight with Scott? The gentle touch of his hands. The lean strength of his body.

She spent the nights dreaming about him. The sound of his voice. His slow smile. The feel of his arms around her. She woke up clutching her pillow and burning inside.

She packed and repacked. Planned outfits and then discarded them. Never had she been so conscious of her appearance. Never had she so desperately wanted to look her best.

She called Trisha to tell her about San Antonio and the "assignment," and caught herself babbling about Casey and how she was sure the girl would find him interesting.

"Can I tell momma you're going to meet a man?" Trisha asked with excitement.

"No," Paige answered quickly. "I'm not really going to meet him. I'm just going to do a story on him. There's a big difference."

The girl was disappointed.

Paige promised to bring her souvenirs and possibly even a pair of cowboy boots, and her mood changed back to one of excitement.

Paige hung up the phone and smiled to herself. She *was* going to meet a man. It was too soon in the tenuous relationship to make a public statement of the true reason for her trip, but the truth of it was never out of her mind. She was going to meet Casey and the reasons had nothing to do with research.

The night before her trip she frantically ran to a huge shopping mall and dashed from store to store, searching for something. She didn't quite know what, but something to make her attractive . . . something to give her the confidence she so desperately needed. Nothing she owned seemed right anymore.

Finally the day dawned. She awoke with the sun and spent hours fidgeting over her hair and deciding and redeciding on the outfit she would wear.

Suitcases in tow, she arrived at the airport early. The airline people took forever to announce boarding. She was first in line, first to find her seat, first to buckle herself in.

Was she making a mistake? Was she blindly rushing into a heartbreak? Was she risking too much? She leaned back as the airliner roared down the runway and lifted into the sky. It was too late to back out now. She was committed. In just a matter of hours she would see Casey Cavanaugh face to face.

## Chapter Seven

The airliner touched down in San Antonio at 11:00 A.M. Texas time, 9:00 California time. Hard to believe it was almost the lunch hour here. She hadn't even had her breakfast yet. Paige stood up in the aisle—and spilled the contents of her purse all over the orange carpet. Her hands shook as she gathered up the assorted odds and ends. She felt like a wreck. The sleepless nights were taking their toll.

She glanced at her watch again as she followed the slowly moving line off the plane. Less than two hours till Casey's arrival. Could she possibly pull herself together in that amount of time?

She rushed to the car-rental desk and arranged for a small economy car for the week. She claimed her baggage and nabbed a porter to wheel it out to the little green car. Quickly she asked directions and then navigated the short distance to the private aviation facilities. She parked at the main building and scouted the place. Yes, she could drive out to the aircraft tie-down area to load her party's baggage after he parked. Yes, they had radio contact with incoming aircraft and could alert her as to Casey's arrival. And most important, yes, they had a ladies' lounge.

She descended upon the ladies' room with a bulging tote bag and an urgent desire to look her best, fast. She scrubbed her face clean and redid her eyes and cheeks and lips with the utmost care. She brushed her hair till it gleamed, and twisted and pinned it with tortoiseshell combs. She changed her blouse and added a gold chain. She pulled on her favorite blazer and then surveyed herself in the mirror.

If only her eyes weren't tinged with red. If only she weren't so thin. Would he notice? How would he react to her now? Would he still be attracted to her or would he be disappointed—or worse, disinterested—when he saw her?

She sprayed her hair and neck with a fine mist of perfume. She was ready. Her whole body trembled with excitement as she repacked the tote and walked back out to the car.

The weather was clear, and a gentle sun shone down on her. She unbuttoned the wool blazer and debated whether to take it off. The morning was warming fast, but she was convinced that she looked better with the jacket on, and she wanted Casey to see her in it. To start with, anyway.

Had she ever been this nervous or excited about

seeing a man? For that matter, had she ever been this nervous or excited about anything? She felt almost ridiculous. Grown women weren't supposed to act this way! Grown women had both feet planted firmly on the ground. She wondered if she was losing her sense of reality.

What would happen now? Not just today, but over the course of the week? Would they be able to overcome their stormy beginnings? Could a relationship be built out of their attraction for each other, or was that all they would ever have—mutual attraction?

And did she even want a relationship? Was the Casey that had burned in her mind and haunted her dreams for weeks just a fantasy—a fairy-tale character she had created to rationalize or excuse the very real physical attraction the man held for her? She had to get control of herself. She had to evaluate this man anew. She had to coolly and objectively determine just who Casey Cavanaugh was, what her feelings were for him, and what, if anything, he felt for her.

She stood on the concrete and watched the silver-and-black single-engine plane land and taxi to the parking ramp. She started across the open area toward it. As the craft swung wide and then jockeyed into position over the tie-down ropes she saw the crimson CC emblazoned on the tail.

She stopped, knees suddenly shaky, palms damp. She'd known it was him, known the colors of his plane, known he was in a landing pattern, but somehow seeing those two interlocking initials made his presence so much more immediate, so much more real.

The engine noise died and the propeller wound down, rapidly changing from a whirling circle of movement to a single stationary blade. Three airport employees in matching coveralls rushed into position, each grabbing the end of a rope imbedded in the asphalt and threading the free end through the metal loops beneath the wings and tail of the craft.

The door opened and Paige held her breath. Any minute now, any minute she would see him. She squeezed her eyes shut and forced herself to take several deep breaths. When she opened her eyes he was there, climbing out. He straightened and stood a moment on the wing. The rising sun at his back made him look somehow invincible, like the hero in an old movie.

He swung down off the wing with a casual ease and spoke to the coveralled men. She couldn't distinguish the words, but she saw them all laugh, saw the men look up at Casey from their kneeling positions at the ropes as though they worshipped him.

He turned and saw her. He stood there a moment as though surprised, and Paige was struck with conflicting urges—to run away from him and to run to him. Her heart raced, and she could feel the pulse points in her neck and hear the roaring in her ears.

He started toward her and she watched him come, frozen to the spot like some doomed creature. His hat was a soft gray this time. His shirt a steel blue with wine. The sun caught his gold buckle and watch and glinted off them in shards of light that burned her eyes.

She searched frantically for words. What would she say? What could she say?

He stopped in silence before her. Slowly he took off his dark green aviator's glasses. The fine tracing of a new scar lined the corner of his eye. His gaze swept over her face, and then their eyes locked in a sudden, almost violent embrace. She gave herself completely to the dark-blue intensity, and he took her without question. The shock of it made her weak, but she didn't falter. She opened up, reached out, responded in ways she'd never dreamed possible.

And still they hadn't touched or spoken.

"Casey," a voice called. "Did you want us to top your tanks?"

The spell was broken. He turned his head to answer. Paige swallowed hard and tried to gather the pieces of herself together. She looked down, the only safe direction, and saw that instead of boots, he wore brightly colored jogging shoes with his sharply creased jeans. The discovery struck her as funny and brought her back to some sort of precarious mental balance.

"I like your shoes," she said. "Purple has always been one of my favorites."

He turned back to her and grinned, a heart-stopping, devilishly boyish grin, accented by those wonderful deep crescents at the corners of his mouth.

"Do you have a car?" he asked.

"Yes," she said, grateful for something concrete to latch on to, some purpose to set her mind on. "I'll go get it while you unload your things."

Before he could answer, she spun and hurried for the car.

She tried to be casual as she helped him load his gear into the green compact. Casual comments. Casual actions. She dropped his briefcase and slammed the car door on his gear-bag strap. She tore her stocking and broke two nails getting into the car. She ground the gears miserably and jerked and lunged in first. So much for casual.

"I made reservations at the Holiday," she said cautiously. "We hadn't discussed it but...."

"I always stay at the river Hilton," he declared shortly

"Oh, certainly...if you have someplace you'd rather stay that will be fine.... I just thought...it might be easier...working together might be easier...if we were in the same hotel."

"You're right," he agreed. "That's why I made you reservations at the Hilton, too."

"Oh," she said, heart hammering in her chest.

"Strictly in the interest of business," he added.

"Of course," she agreed quickly.

"Is this the best you could do for a car?" he asked, shifting in his seat and readjusting the piece of luggage at his feet.

"I was trying to be economical," she said in defense of her choice.

"You could have rented bicycles," he said with a smirk that made her want to slam on the brakes and order him out.

"You could have arranged for your own car," she said with a lightness she didn't feel.

"Oh, no," he insisted sarcastically. "I agreed to include the press in everything I do at this rodeo. Separate vehicles would not be in the spirit of the agreement."

He disliked her. The sudden certainty was like a

physical blow. It was in his voice and in the closed, wary darkness of his eyes. She must have imagined everything at the parking area. She must have wanted it so badly that she had imagined him reaching out, imagined him responding, imagined him mirroring and returning all her emotions. The man plainly and simply disliked her. And she could hardly blame him. It was her own fault. He had been interested in her once, but she had destroyed his interest. She had no chance now with Casey. She had no business being in San Antonio. Her stomach felt leaden and heavy.

He was polite but distant on the remainder of the ride across town. He was silent as they unloaded their luggage. He ignored her during the registration process. By the time she stood outside her door, fumbling the key into the lock, she was in a haze of misery and close to tears.

"I need to leave in about fifteen minutes."

His voice made her jump. He was opening the door next to hers.

"What?" she said, hating herself for sounding so dumb and slow.

"I've got an appointment. I need to leave in about fifteen minutes," he said with the exaggerated clarity of an adult repeating something to a child. "You said you wanted to tag along on everything. Fine. Be ready in fifteen minutes. Otherwise tell me now, so I can call a cab."

"I'll be ready," she answered weakly, and pushed open her door.

Why had she come? It was perfectly obvious what Casey Cavanaugh thought of her—nothing! Her misery shifted to anger. She was acting like a lovesick teenager—running halfway across the country after a man. How could she have been so stupid? How could she have allowed her emotions to completely overpower her intellect? If she had only ignored the burning inside her. If she had only disregarded the dreams of him at night and the visions of him that hovered at the edge of her consciousness during the day. If she had only been her calm, practical self, this mistake would never have happened. What in the world was wrong with her?

Casey Cavanaugh was very probably as bad as she had first thought him to be. He was probably just as arrogant and conceited as she had first thought. She had been building him up in her imagination until the person she'd come to Texas to see was someone who probably didn't exist in reality. Her sense of judgment had very likely been right on target in the beginning.

Casey shut the door to his room and stalked into the bathroom. He turned on the faucet full force and splashed cold water on his face. Damn that woman! Why had she done this? Why had she arranged all this? And why on earth had he ever agreed to it?

Just being near her was torture. The way she spoke. The way she moved. The way the sun lit up her hair. Why was he subjecting himself to this? Had he imagined it would be different this time? Had he forgotten that she had some kind of impenetrable shield around her? Had he forgotten that nothing could break through that icy reserve of hers?

At the airport, just for a minute he had thought...

imagined probably... that there was something. Some kind of emotional current between them. Some kind of shared feelings. How stupid. Why couldn't he just give up and admit defeat? But, then, that wasn't the problem. He could—and in fact, had—admitted defeat. Getting her out of his mind was the hard part.

It was going to be a long week. A very long week. But he would just have to make the best of it. Just play it by ear and not let her get to him. Maybe they could at least learn to be friends. He both admired and respected her. Maybe out of all this he could at least salvage a friendship.

Paige showered and changed into lightweight slacks and a crisp, teal cotton shirt. She surveyed her hair in the mirror. With three minutes left there were not a lot of possibilities. And anyway, what did it matter how she looked? She pulled her hair back to the nape and secured it with a large barrette, added a touch of lip gloss and headed for the door.

The appointment was not at all what she'd expected. After a quick hamburger they went straight to the children's ward of a large hospital. Two men, local representatives of a service organization, were there waiting for Casey. They were all smiles and repeated thanks for his "being so generous with his time."

Paige couldn't help but suspect that Casey had set the entire episode up for her benefit to ensure a good image for himself in whatever she wrote. He must have arranged the little hospital bit right after he agreed to "cooperate" with the press!

By late afternoon they had visited three children's

wards, and she was exhausted. She had long since stopped taking pictures, and had resorted to simply leaving her trusty cassette on Record and relaxing in a corner chair. Casey, on the other hand, seemed indefatigable.

She watched him reach out to the children. A pat here, a squeeze there, a manly handshake with a five-year-old. The children loved him. They crowded in, talking and chattering, reaching for his buckle, climbing on his lap, basking in his quiet strength.

Paige had to admit that it was touching. Even if he was faking it for the sake of his story image, the children were still benefiting. And maybe, just maybe, he wasn't faking. Maybe Casey Cavanaugh was the genuine article. Her mind spun in confusion.

One of the men from the service organization pulled a chair up next to her and sat down. "He's quite a guy, isn't he," the man remarked with awe in his voice.

"The children certainly seem to think so," Paige replied carefully.

"Yup," the man agreed, and then chuckled. "And they always do."

"Always?" Paige knit her brows in question.

"It's the same every year," the man answered, shifting his heavy bulk in the chair. "They're always crazy about him."

"You mean he's done this before?"

"Sure. This'll be his fourth year. We've tried to get some other cowboys, but nobody will ever come a day early the way Casey does. Nobody else is willing to give that much time."

Casey began singing the children a rodeo song about a mean Brahma bull. The group was enthralled.

Guilt washed over Paige. Casey was a good man, a kind man, and she *was* trying to cast him as a villain. Could it be that she was mentally working at discrediting him in order to ease the pain of his rejection? That she was subconsciously protecting herself from hurt by convincing herself that he was a man who was unworthy of her affection and thus not worth feeling hurt over?

She looked across the room at Casey, his dark-blue eyes so full of warmth and affection for the children, and she felt a cloud of pure misery envelop her. That beautiful, wonderful man had been interested in her once—she had had a chance with him once—and she'd thrown it all away.

The following days were a whirlwind of activity. She followed him to autograph sessions and speaking engagements and meetings where people proposed every manner of promotional scheme to him. And of course she followed him to the rodeo to watch him ride.

Paige didn't feel as though she'd had a moment's rest since arriving in Texas. In a fog she drove the little car across San Antonio toward the river Hilton. She was both mentally and physically exhausted from the long hours and the strain of Casey's silent, distant presence. Tonight she simply didn't care. She didn't care that he rode the whole way without saying a word to her. She was too tired. Nothing mattered. She just didn't care anymore.

"What time tomorrow?" she asked bleakly as they walked into the Hilton lobby.

"You can sleep in tomorrow," Casey answered with a look of amusement.

It was clear that he didn't think Paige could take any more of the grueling schedule.

"It doesn't make any difference to me," Paige flared. "I can be ready to go as early as I need to be." She pushed the elevator button harder than necessary.

He nodded and grinned the same grin that had always caused her heart to skip. The realization that it still did was painful.

She stepped into the elevator and pressed herself against the cool, smooth side. Was it her imagination, or was he warmer, more attentive?

He grinned again. "Let's just say I need to sleep in tomorrow, then. You can get up whenever you want. Give me a call about eleven."

Paige nodded and pulled her room key from her purse. She felt suddenly self-conscious, unsure. Where did she stand with Casey Cavanaugh? Was there any chance...?

The sun streamed into the room through a patch of glass not quite covered by drapery. Paige stretched and turned over to look at her watch on the nightstand. Ten o'clock! She had been completely out for nine hours!

Casey. Awareness brought him sharply to mind. His face. His eyes. The span of his shoulders. The broad strength of his hands.

Throughout the past days she had tried to convince herself that she felt nothing, that she could turn off all thoughts of him, that she could rationally and practically accept his lack of interest and put him completely out of her mind. Now suddenly she could see her denial of feelings for what it was—a miserable failure. If anything her awareness of Casey had been heightened by the time she'd spent with him in San Antonio.

Quickly Paige went through her morning routine. She French-braided her hair from a side part and wove the shining braid into a knot at her nape. She wanted to look special today. Even if he didn't notice... even if he didn't care... She dressed and added perfume at her neck and wrists.

With time to spare she tried to force herself to work. She sat down at the typewriter and willed her fingers to create words. None came. Her mind wandered back to Casey. What plans did he have today? Why had he been so evasive about today's schedule? What was on his mind? Did he ever think about her? Did he ever wonder....?

With a start she realized it was past eleven. Eagerly she reached for the phone to call him. But why phone? His room was just next door.

He answered after one knock. Was it possible... did he seem glad to see her?

"Good morning," she said brightly, realizing as she spoke that he was dressed differently today. The casual knit shirt, jogging shoes and baseball cap looked almost foreign on him. If she hadn't been certain of his identity she would never have believed he was a famous rodeo star. The change had a relaxing effect on her. He was certainly less intimidating this way.

Everything about him seemed different today. The looks he gave her. The words so intensely spoken. Even the way he insisted on driving. She didn't allow herself to consider what it all meant. The day was much too beautiful and lazily warm to spoil it with thinking. She settled into the passenger seat and leaned her head back in pure enjoyment.

"What's on the agenda today?" she asked with half-closed eyes.

"Valentine's Day," he said simply, and kept his eyes on the road.

She smiled to herself. He was right. She'd completely forgotten it was Valentine's Day. "So it is," she said. "But what's that got to do with your schedule? They don't close the town for the event, do they?

"Probably not," he said in mock seriousness. "But I feel it's unpatriotic to ignore traditional American holidays. As good citizens we're obligated to celebrate Valentine's Day and put aside all thoughts of work."

"Are you serious?" she asked incredulously.

He looked at her as though offended.

"You are serious!" Paige struggled to regain her composure. 'All right," she agreed in a businesslike tone. "But first let's do something about lunch. I skipped breakfast and I'm starving."

Casey didn't say another word until they pulled into a downtown parking lot.

"Mexican food okay?" he asked.

"Fine," Paige replied, and climbed quickly out of the car.

Casa Rio, the sign read. They walked down the stairs from street level to the river walk below.

"Outside all right?" Casey asked.

She nodded, and he led the way to a Spanish-tile-topped table beside the water. Paige was awed. She had had no idea that this charming scene existed beneath the bustle of downtown San Antonio.

The river itself was confined to a canal about twenty feet wide. Walkways meandered beside it punctuated by little stone bridges, waterfalls and lush tropical greenery. Casey explained that the restaurants and the little shops she could see from her vantage point were arranged so that their downstairs back doors faced the river, while their upstairs front doors opened out onto the downtown streets. It was an ingenious arrangement.

"How far does the river go?" she asked in wonder.

"I don't know exactly," Casey replied. "I know that it winds around down here for several miles. We'll take a boat ride later and find out."

Paige loved good Mexican food and was intrigued by the difference between the type of cooking in Texas versus her native California variety. She stuffed herself on hot, freshly made corn tortillas, spicy salsa blended from ripe tomatoes and peppers; smooth guacamole; tender chunks of beef in red chili gravy; and wonderful homemade tamales wrapped in corn husks.

When she was too full to eat anymore, she pushed her chair back and threw bits of leftover tortilla to the greedy pigeons cooing on the sidewalk. Conversation had been minimal up to this point. Now that her hunger was satisfied, her mind was full of questions.

Why did Casey suggest this kind of day? Why did he suggest spending this kind of day with her?

He could have found any number of people to spend a day like this with—people whose company he enjoyed. Why would he elect to waste his relaxation hours with her? On the days when he was forced to work with her she knew that he only tolerated her presence for the sake of the magazine article.

Most confusing of all was the effect he was having on her. She felt completely at ease, as though she were with a friend. As though they had somehow established a rapport, a comfortable togetherness.

"You look so different today," she commented as she fed the last of the tortilla to the flock of birds and brushed the crumbs from her hands.

He shrugged and stared down at the rippling jade water. "Somedays I feel like being plain old John C. Cavanaugh. No autographs, no shaking hands with strangers, no big deals. Today's just one of those days."

Paige studied him a moment, uncertain as to the extent of his sincerity. "I didn't know you ever got tired of being the big star."

His eyes drifted back to her and one corner of his mouth curved up in a lazy half grin. "There's a lot you don't know about me."

"All right," she challenged. "We've got all afternoon. Tell me something I don't know about you."

His eyes searched hers a moment, and her breath caught under the dark intensity of his gaze. Suddenly he looked back down at the sun-sparkled water and laughed.

"Sorry, no interviews today. Not even to beautiful lady writers."

A thrill ran through Paige and left her feeling slightly giddy. He thought she was beautiful! Casey Cavanaugh actually thought she was beautiful.

She felt an overwhelming need to know more about this man. A man she had seen as rude and arrogant and self-centered. A man who had angered and embarrassed her. A man she had since learned to be intelligent and kind and supremely generous. And, through it all, a man she found to be exciting and compelling and intensely attractive.

"Strictly off the record," she promised, smiling and crossing her heart in the age-old childish ritual.

He laughed. A laugh that conveyed more than pleasure. A laugh that showered her with warmth and acceptance and trust. Her heart soared and she felt marvelously light and gay.

"Your name," she said, "I thought it was Casey, but you just said John C." There was so very much she wanted to know about him. So very much.

"Well, since it's strictly off the record..." he said in mock hesitancy. "My legal name is John Casey Cavanaugh III. My grandfather answers to John and my dad to J.C., so they hung the Casey on me. My family used to worry about what they'd use on my son... if I ever had one. What they'd stick on little J.C.C. IV for a handle." He shrugged and grinned. "They've pretty much given up on any fourths in the family, though. My mom's decided I'm just not the marryin' kind."

"Is she right?" Paige asked impulsively, and then toyed with her napkin in a fit of self-consciousness.

"Maybe," Casey said. "Or maybe I just haven't met the right person. I've been so zeroed in on my rodeo career that I haven't had time to do much looking. . . . And, well, the women you meet on the road. . . they're the kind a guy never gets serious about. Most of them are either groupies or other guys' wives."

There was an uncomfortable silence between them.

"Hey," he said, changing the mood completely. "I saw a copy of your first article, the one you were working on at Denver. It was good. You really captured the flavor of it all."

"It's not even in print yet," Paige remarked in complete surprise. "How in the world could you have seen it?"

"Contacts," Casey said, raising his eyebrows and winking. "I've got lots of contacts."

"I'm glad you liked it. It was my first attempt at a big project," Paige admitted sheepishly.

"You should really be proud, then," Casey said quietly. "It was a first-class job."

Paige stared down at the water, perilously close to tears. His praise touched her deeply. His sincerity overwhelmed her. Finally she swallowed the lump in her throat and looked up at him. All barriers were down. He was so totally open. So vulnerable. She tried to smile, but the moment was not made for smiling.

A stirring began deep inside her and grew to a warm, breathless glow. She stood quickly, confused and flustered and trying hard to hide it.

"How about that boat ride you mentioned," she said, fumbling for her purse.

They walked together, close but not touching,

down the river toward the boat dock. Paige experienced a feeling of rightness, a sense of well-being that she hadn't felt since childhood. Everything was so perfect. The distant roar of the waterfall, the endless ripple and flow of the river at her feet. The gentle sun casting lacy patterns as it filtered down through the trees. And the man beside her. The man so close beside her.

Boat tickets purchased, they sat on a stone bench to wait. Their conversation was pleasant, comforting and insignificant. She was so aware of his physical presence that his every move seemed magnified. His arm flung casually across the bench behind her shoulders took on major importance. The spot where their thighs almost touched became a burning point on her skin.

"It's here," he said, and stood up.

She rose and moved beside him into the small knot of people lining up at the docking point. The flat open boat looked like a river barge fitted with railings and padded benches.

The line moved forward. He took her arm as they started down the stone steps, and she had the insane desire to become totally helpless, to need everything from him—his jacket about her shoulders; his strong hands opening doors; his arm about her waist, steadying, guiding. It was an incredibly unfamiliar and strange sensation, and Paige wasn't sure how to deal with it.

The boat filled fast, and they were pushed closer and closer together on the orange vinyl bench as stragglers arrived and squeezed into place. Their bodies pressed together, touching in what seemed like a hundred heated places.

She tried to concentrate on the moving scenery as they chugged downstream—the old buildings, the picturesque walkways, the lush foliage, the fountain and turnaround that marked the 1968 location of the San Antonio HemisFair—but she found it increasingly difficult to focus her attention on anything but that hard muscular thigh pressing against hers.

Water splashed against the sides of the boat and sprayed across her arm. A breeze stirred, blowing across her wet skin and chilling her. She shivered slightly and crossed her arms tightly against her chest.

"Cold?" he asked, and without waiting for an answer, quickly put his arm around her shoulders and hugged her toward him.

She sat perfectly still, drinking in the sensations—the strength, the warmth, the total feeling of security that arm gave her. Beside the boat, darting fish gleamed and danced through the green water. She watched them, afraid to look up or shift position even slightly, afraid he might move his arm away.

Too soon the ride was over. In silence they strolled down the river walk and across a water spill. The sound and spray from water coursing over stones filled the air.

"There's lots to see in this town." Casey said. "Are you up for any sight-seeing?"

Paige agreed quickly, and he led her back up to the street level and over to La Villita, a restored part of the old city. For hours they poked through the tiny shops and each time their arms brushed, each time their eyes met, she felt the stirring.

They strolled through the Alamo complex and

stopped to watch the film dealing with the true history of the battle and the errors in judgment that had sent so many men to their deaths. Paige was amazed at how much Casey knew about the whole incident.

"How did you learn so much history?" she asked.

"It was my major in college," he said, pausing to study an artifact in a glass case. "And I still get carried away with it once in a while." He sounded almost apologetic. "It's all so fascinating though... the facts behind events... the underlying reasons for the power struggles... the human frailties that brought about or changed the course of history.

"That's what it all comes down to, you know— human frailties, human beings. History isn't just statistics. It's human beings—individuals who rose above the crowd, who shaped their own destinies and, in the process, the destinies of thousands."

He paused for a moment and stared off at some unseen point, deep in thought.

"One man," he continued, "That's all it takes. One man, or woman, who understands his or her own possibilities, his or her own potential, and refuses to buckle under. One determined person who ignores convention, who goes against all odds... that's history."

He stopped talking, and, as though coming out of a trance, suddenly looked at her and his surroundings self-consciously. Abruptly he cleared his throat and moved on to the next display case.

Paige stared after him in wonder. How many facets did this man have? How many more sides were there to Casey Cavanaugh?

She watched him move away. His head was down and his eyes were skimming over the displays instead of studying them. Both his expression and his manner told her he was trying to retreat. He had gone too far, had exposed feelings ordinarily kept hidden, and now he was trying to protect himself by establishing some distance and closing up.

Paige's heart swelled with a host of emotions. She wanted to reassure him, to share the feelings with him, to open up to him in return.

"Casey."

He turned toward her, his expression guarded.

"You're that kind of man," she said softly. "A man who goes against all odds. A man who makes history."

His dark eyes narrowed. Had she made a mistake? Her breath came short and shallow. Then gradually his expression softened and warmed. He said nothing. Words were inadequate. Feelings passed between them that could never be expressed in words.

"Time to close folks," a voice announced loudly.

Casey glanced at his watch and then started toward the door. Paige watched him go, unable to move, still under the spell of the moment. He turned back toward her and stopped. He said nothing, but his eyes met hers in a timeless look that said everything. Then he held out his hand to her—simply, unconditionally, held out his hand.

Never had a single gesture affected her so profoundly.

Hand in hand they walked back toward the car, back across the city streets and down stone steps to river level. Tiny jewellike lights winked on in the twilight. They filled the trees and outlined the shadowy buildings. The cooing of the pigeons softened. The first star appeared, and she silently wished for the afternoon not to end.

"I'm up tonight on my bull," Casey said. "And I need to get back to the room and get ready, but maybe... maybe after the rodeo we could have a late dinner?"

He said it as a question. He said it with hope and uncertainty.

She wanted to cry, "Yes, yes, yes," and grab both his hands and dance around in a circle under the twinkling lights. She wanted to throw back her head and laugh out loud. She wanted to jump in a fountain like Zelda and shout her happiness to the world.

"Yes, I'd like that," she said quietly.

## Chapter Eight

Paige dressed hurriedly for the rodeo. She knew how important it was for Casey to get there in time to prepare himself mentally as well as physically for the contest. Above all, she didn't want to be the cause of him arriving late. That would be far worse than not looking perfect. When the knock came at her door she knew it was him, and she was glad she'd hurried.

"I'm all ready," she said as she opened the door. "Just need to find my tape recorder..."

He stepped into the room and her words trailed off without finish. He wore a pale gray shirt of fine starched cotton and a snug, dark, leather vest that made her acutely aware of the width of his shoulders and span of his chest tapering down to the hard, leanness of his hips and thighs. The gray hat he had on cast shadows across the chiseled planes and angles of his face.

The darkness of his eyes changed and softened at the sight of her, and she felt a surge of almost overwhelming need. She wanted him. She wanted to touch him and feel him warm against her. She wanted to be held by him, to be wrapped in his arms so tightly that nothing could break them apart.

In the slow-motion sequence of a dream she watched him toss the jacket he carried on a chair. His eyes locked on hers as he took off the gray hat and walked toward her. One step. Two steps. The sound of her heart's wild beating filled her ears.

He cupped her face in his strong hands and stared down into her eyes. Her breath caught and held in her chest. *Kiss me, please kiss me*, she pleaded silently.

His lips were soft and warm and gentle against hers. The wonderful sweetness of the kiss swelled inside her and fueled the fire stirring, smoldering, deep within her. She reached out, wrapping her arms around his neck, pulling him closer.

He responded fiercely, holding her so tight against him that she could feel the heat from every inch of his body. She wound her fingers into the soft waves of his hair and buried her face in his neck, breathing in the clean smell of soap from his skin.

The kiss was mutual this time. She sought his lips as eagerly as he sought hers. And there was suddenly no end, no stopping point, just a growing urgency, a raw passionate need building inside her.

Roughly he pulled away, holding her at arm's length, his breathing as ragged as her own. "I still have to ride tonight," he said. His words were filled with regret. "But later, after the rodeo..."

She nodded, unable to trust her voice, unable to

think of any appropriate words. In a daze she found her recorder and followed him through the door. If he hadn't been there to watch her she would have stopped to stare at herself in the mirror. Surely the change was visible. She was a new person. A different person. For the first time in her life she knew what it meant to truly feel like a woman.

Casey drove through the streets of San Antonio like a man pursued. He had to get control of himself. He had to block her from his mind. He had a bull to ride tonight. But there she was, sitting beside him in the car, so beautiful and warm and inviting. He didn't dare look at her. He didn't dare get lost again in those green eyes.

He could hardly believe his good fortune. How could this all be happening when he had given up completely and was just trying to be friends? How had he gotten so lucky? What had he done to deserve the way she looked at him now? The way her eyes shone when he entered a room. The way her voice softened when she spoke to him. What wonderful thing had happened to make her care for him?

He pulled into the coliseum parking lot and unloaded his gear. *Get your mind on the bull,* he cautioned himself, *get your mind on your ride.* But here she was, walking beside him, so soft and touchable and so close that he could smell a hint of her perfume. He had never felt so helpless in his life.

Paige floated through the first part of the rodeo. She was barely aware of the happenings around her.

Events were announced and took place and concluded without her knowledge. The lights went out and a singer appeared in the arena standing in a circle of light. Time for the entertainer, she thought vaguely, but didn't hear any of the songs.

Her mind was full of Casey. Her lips still throbbed from his kisses. Her body still felt the heat of him pressing against her. The rodeo would soon be over and they would be together. They would be together with the entire night stretching before them.

The clatter and bang of the bulls being loaded into the chutes brought Paige sharply back to reality. This was Casey's event. And there he was, stepping out from behind the chutes. He moved with a fluid grace, stretching, bending, warming his muscles, preparing his body for the contest ahead. The light glinted off his midnight-and-silver chaps. Bull-riding chaps, he'd explained to her. Entirely different from his red ones, which were bronc-riding chaps. Bull-riding chaps had to be cut shorter and with less flare at the bottoms. They had to be designed specifically to run in. A cowboy couldn't afford to get tangled in his chaps when he was trying to escape the murderous rage of a charging bull.

She was so proud of him. He had so much courage and determination and skill. Instead of an arrogant show-off, she now saw him as a man putting forth the supreme effort, forcing his mind and body to go beyond their limits. He was the best. But that distinction hadn't come easily to him. He drove himself unmercifully to earn every title, every distinction.

She leaned forward in her seat as he climbed the

chute to set his rope on the brown-and-black-speckled monster. The bull tossed his horns and lunged repeatedly against the confining planks. Calmly and purposefully Casey set his rope and climbed down onto the bull's back. He worked his gloved hand into the braided-rope handhold and held his free arm in the air.

The announcer went on and on about Casey and his greatness and his accomplishments. Paige's stomach had butterflies and her knuckles were white from clenching her fists. Casey nodded and the chute gate swung open. Paige held her breath.

The huge animal exploded into the arena, twisting and turning and jumping in both directions. One minute Casey was sitting there pretty as a picture, and the next minute he was in trouble. He fought for a hold with his feet and he threw his body and worked his free arm, but nothing could keep him from slipping down into the inside of that animal's spin.

Paige stood, covering her mouth with both hands. All around her the crowd shouted and screamed. Everything took on a slow-motion quality—the bull's deadly spinning, Casey's frantic efforts to pull his hand loose from the rope and the clown's futile attempts at help. In the well. Paige remembered hearing the cowboys talk about the disastrous consequences of bucking off into the center of a spinning bull's movement. They called it the "well."

Casey was limp now, hanging, flopping like a rag doll from the angry bull. The animal leaped into the air and out of the spin, throwing his head back, aiming a horn at the man still attached by one arm to his back. He caught Casey full in the chest and slung him up and out. The cowboy fell in a crumpled pile and the bull turned back, head down, deadly horns in attack position. He ran full tilt at Casey, catching him again on a horn and tossing him into the air like a rubber toy.

Cowboys ran in from the sidelines, and two men on horseback rushed forward. Along with the clowns they converged on the menacing bull and distracted him long enough for Casey to be dragged to safety.

Paige leaped to her feet and ran blindly toward the stairs. By the time she made her way down, they had carried him from the arena on a stretcher and were backing the ambulance into position in preparation for loading him. She stopped, frozen in place by the heart-wrenching sight of Casey on the stretcher. His shirt was torn and he was covered with dirt and blood. They streaked his face and matted his hair and blotched his arms and chest.

Tears ran down her cheeks unchecked as she slowly took the last few steps and knelt by his side.

"How is he?" she asked the paramedic in a choked voice she hardly recognized as her own.

Before the man could answer her, Casey moaned and opened his eyes.

"He's comin' out of it," the paramedic called to his partner, who was directing the ambulance.

"What's going on?" Casey demanded in a hoarse whisper. He struggled to sit up, but the paramedic had fastened the straps on the stretcher and they held him fast.

"Don't!" Paige cried, desperately afraid he would injure himself further.

"Take it easy, buddy," the paramedic said. "We'll have you loaded up and on the way in no time."

"No," Casey insisted, and struggled again against the straps. "No ambulance rides. No doctors. I'm fine. Let me off this thing."He winced with the pain of his efforts.

"It's your decision fella, but I'm tellin' ya, you need a doctor—and right now."

Casey shook his head and the paramedic reached for the strap release.

Paige couldn't stand it any longer. She leaned over him, pushing the medic away, and gently brushed the hair back away from his forehead. Her tears fell on his face and mixed with the grime and the blood.

"Please," she begged him. "Please. I couldn't stand it if anything happened to you. Please let them take care of you." She sobbed involuntarily. "Please."

He looked at her for a moment, and she saw in his eyes that he would do as she asked.

"All right," he told the paramedic, "but only if she comes with me."

Paige crawled into the ambulance and sat beside him. His eyes narrowed with pain and then closed. *Please let him be all right*, Paige repeated over and over in a silent prayer. She stroked his forehead and cheeks and held his hand. Anxiously she watched the medic's face every time the man took Casey's vital signs.

The siren wailed in a continuous, nerve-shattering cadence. How much farther could the hospital possibly be, she wondered. He looked so pale beneath the coating of grime and his breathing sounded labored and harsh.

The medic reexamined him and frowned. Immediately he set up an intravenous injection. Paige swallowed hard but the lump in her throat wouldn't move. She squeezed her eyes shut against the sight of the needle plunging into Casey's arm.

Finally, after what seemed like an eternity, they reached the hospital. They backed into place and the doors opened and men and women in white surrounded them and took charge. Casey was poked and prodded and swiftly transferred to a gurney. She followed them inside the big automatic double doors leading into the emergency room and then watched helplessly as they wheeled him around a corner and out of sight.

"Are you a relative?"

The voice startled her, and she turned to find a thin, redheaded nurse with clipboard in hand addressing her.

"No, just a friend."

"Oh," the nurse said in a perfunctory tone of complete dismissal. She spun on her heel and started off down the hall.

"Wait!" Paige called after her. "How can I find out how he is? Who can I ask? When will they know something?"

The nurse's manner softened a little. She took a few steps back toward Paige. "I'll try to keep you posted," she said. "You can find me just around the corner at the emergency desk. And if you go around the pop machines there—" she gestured with her clipboard "—you'll find a waiting area."

Paige wandered aimlessly about the cramped room. She was alone amid the black vinyl couches and the low formica tables piled with year-old magazines. She stood and sat and stood again.

What was taking so long? Surely they knew the extent of his injuries by now. He might not be hurt badly at all. Hadn't he told her that most arena injuries look worse than they actually are? Then again, what if... No, she scolded herself. There was no use conjuring up problems, imagining things to worry about. She would wait until she had the findings, wait until she knew the precise diagnosis, to start any serious worrying.

She hated to bother the nurse, but she couldn't stand it any longer. She had to ask. Hesitantly she approached the emergency desk. The redheaded nurse had her head down and was writing something on a medical chart.

"May I help you?" an unfamiliar nurse asked.

"I'm waiting for her," Paige said, indicating the redhead.

At the sound of Paige's voice the woman raised her eyes from her chart. "I was just coming out to talk to you," she said, and filed the chart carefully away.

Paige held her breath. Something was wrong. Why didn't the woman just say, "He's fine," or "He'll be ready to go in no time, "or "He just needs a few stitches," or even "We're going to have to keep him overnight for observation." What was she waiting for? Why was she coming around the counter with such a serious expression, and why was she taking so damn long to say anything?

"Mr. Cavanaugh is on his way to surgery. He had a number of broken ribs and one of them punctured his lung. The lung collapsed."

"Oh, my God," Paige breathed, and sagged against the wall beside her. "What does that mean?"

"It means," said the nurse, "that the collapsed lung must be reexpanded and the doctors are inserting a tube in an effort to accomplish that reexpansion. That is about all I can tell you until after the surgery."

Paige nodded and pressed her clenched fists against her mouth.

"Are you all right?" the woman asked.

Paige nodded again and straightened. Of course she was all right. She had been through much worse than this with her mother. She squared her shoulders and cleared her throat.

"Will you let me know when the surgery is over?" she asked quietly.

The nurse glanced at her watch. "I go off duty before too long, but you can check with anyone at the desk for information."

"How long should I wait before I check?" Paige asked.

"Try back in about an hour."

Paige bought a soft drink from the machine and sipped at it without tasting. She flipped through tattered copies of ancient magazines without seeing the copy. She found the ladies' room and washed her face and hands. Mostly she stared at the clock.

It was a big round clock with a second hand and large bold numbers. It was a clock to be glanced at while passing by...a clock that could be read from a distance. It was not a good clock to stare at. It was too big. The spaces between the numbers were too far apart. The hands took too long to move. She hated the clock.

After fifty-seven minutes and ten seconds had elapsed Paige finally allowed herself to go to the nurses' station. There was a new group of women on duty. The redhead was gone.

"Excuse me," she said anxiously, "is Casey Cavanaugh out of surgery yet?"

"Are you family?" a large blonde asked.

"No," Paige admitted, "I'm a friend. I rode in with him in the ambulance. I've been waiting to hear."

"Do you know anything about Cavanaugh?" the blonde called over her shoulder to a nurse in the office.

"He's in recovery," the woman answered.

Paige waited with her heart in her throat.

"He's in recovery," the blonde repeated. "You can go on up to five. There's a waiting area there and you can ask at the nurses' station for information."

Paige wheeled and ran for the elevator. Why hadn't she been told to wait on five in the first place, she thought. It was a relief to feel irritation for a moment instead of fear.

The nurses at the fifth-floor station had little more to tell her. The surgery had gone well. He was in recovery. The waiting area was to the left.

She sank into a vinyl couch. Turquoise this time, instead of black. She didn't bother with the magazines. They looked suspiciously like the same ones she'd leafed through in emergency.

She closed her eyes and leaned her head back in an effort to ease some of the tension in her neck. Maybe, when she opened her eyes, it would all be gone. She would wake up in her room at the Hilton and find out this had all been a terrible dream.

Maybe everything was a dream. Even the good parts. Maybe this whole day had never happened. Certainly the afternoon had been dreamlike. And when he'd kissed her in the room—that could easily have been a dream. It had been far too wonderful to be real.

She opened her eyes and looked at her watch. A respectable amount of time had passed since she'd last questioned the nurses. She pushed herself wearily out of the low couch and headed again for the desk.

"Is Casey Cavanaugh still in recovery?" she asked the first person who looked up.

The nurse consulted a paper. "He's been moved to intensive care," she said.

"How is he doing?" Paige asked hopefully. "Can I see him?"

"He's in critical condition," the woman answered evenly. "No visitors except immediate family. Are you family?"

Paige shook her head no and swallowed and blinked to control the tears that were burning in her eyes.

"How soon...will you know something?" she managed to ask.

"His condition could change at any time," the nurse said. "The cafeteria is open for breakfast now. Why don't you go on down and have something to eat. It'll make the time go faster."

Paige nodded and started slowly down the corridor toward the elevators. Breakfast! God, it was morning already. She wasn't hungry, but the nurse was right; doing something would make the time pass more quickly.

The cafeteria was in the basement level. There were no windows. Someone had obviously been concerned with that fact and had tried to compensate for the lack of sunlight by adding huge banks of brilliant fluorescent lighting and painting everything yellow or orange. The harsh white lights and the endless expanses of brightly colored formica gave Paige a feeling of total hopelessness. Someone had tried hard with this room, but it just hadn't worked out. Like her life.

She had always tried so hard and had such good intentions, but somehow nothing ever worked out. As when her mother had gotten sick and Paige had started doing so much around the house. She had wanted to help, to do the right thing, but more than that she had wanted to please her father. He never had been pleased. He'd just expected more and more. And her sisters—she'd wanted to cushion them, to protect them and mother them. They'd ended up nearly hating her for what they saw as her efforts to "smother" them.

She'd tried so hard. She'd wanted to end up like some television family who forges on through tragedy with love and good humor. She'd never meant for her father to take her for granted. She'd never meant for her sisters to resent her. She'd never dreamed that she'd end up with a scattered family who rarely even called. She'd never meant to give up so much of her life for nothing. And that's what it looked like now; all that giving and caring and sacrificing had been for nothing.

After all, what did she have now? A lonely apartment that never heard the sounds of laughter. No close friends, except maybe Judy, and she didn't count, both because she lived so far away and because Judy had been a friend since childhood. Paige had not made one close friend in her adult life.

She liked her job, but she had been so insecure and frightened that she never would have progressed any further had it not been for Maggie Carson's pushing. Her career was the one bright spot in her life right now, but she couldn't take the credit. She couldn't claim to have done even that right. Maggie had had to engineer the entire thing.

Her work with Trisha was positive and good, and she had done that all herself. At least she had something to be proud of. But just lately she had begun to wonder even about that. Something Judy had said had started her thinking, analyzing her relationship with Trisha, and she saw now that she'd been doing more than just helping the girl; she'd been using her as a safe, nonthreatening person to love. She'd been so afraid of adult relationships. She'd been using Trisha as someone to care about without all the dangers and complications.

It was so damn clear to her now! She'd been afraid of everything; friendship, love, career success and yes—even fun. They all involved risks, and she hadn't been brave enough to take them. Just as she hadn't been brave enough to tell her father and sisters, "Hey, I've had enough. We all need to pitch in here to make this family work. I can't be responsible for everything and everyone anymore." She had never been brave enough to say that, because she'd been so afraid of losing their love. Maybe if she had taken that risk... maybe things would be different now. Maybe....

The food on the plastic tray in front of her was cold and unappealing. The smell of it made her queasy. She wrapped the apple in a napkin and slid it into her purse. The remainder she threw away. The hospital was bustling with morning activity as she made her way back to the elevators.

How had she ever been lucky enough to meet Casey? How, when she had been so busy running away from life, when she had tried so hard to keep her head buried in the sand, had she ever met such a wonderful, beautiful, exciting man? And how had he ever seen beneath the icy shell she kept in place for protection? The whole thing was such a miracle that it made her almost believe in Fate—the idea that she and Casey were somehow destined to come into each other's lives.

And now... now there was a chance she might lose him just as swiftly and unpredictably as she'd found him. No! She couldn't believe that would happen. She refused to believe that would happen. He would be fine. He would be healthy and laughing in no time. He had to be.

She stopped at the nurses' station for a report, but there was no change. Again she sat on the turquoise couch. The vinyl was cold and stiff beneath her clothes. She was no longer alone in the waiting area. A middle-aged couple huddled together across the room. As she had walked in she'd heard them complaining about only being allowed ten minutes per visit. *At least you were able to go in,* she found herself thinking.

Her mind twisted and turned through a labyrinth of thoughts. What did all this mean? Were all these realizations, all this new awareness, a gift or a curse? She had not been unhappy before all this—or rather she had never recognized her own unhappiness. Now, understanding all this, she could never go back to what she'd been. She could never live that way again. But did she have the courage to truly change? Was she brave enough to jump into life feet first regardless of the consequences? Specifically, was she brave enough to drop all defenses and open herself up to Casey completely?

She sighed and let her head fall back against the back of the couch. It was all so exhausting, and she was so very, very tired.

She awoke with a start and sat up straight. Someone had said his name. She was certain of it. The middle-aged couple were still across the room, huddled together on a couch. A tall, stoop-shouldered doctor stood in front of them, talking. His voice was deep and weary, and Paige could hear everything he said.

"Your son is going to be fine. The lung has reexpanded and is functioning well. He'll be moved to a private room shortly, and you'll be able to spend as much time as you like with him."

"Oh, thank you, doctor, thank you," the couple breathed in unison.

They were talking about Casey! Those people were Casey's parents.

Paige's first reaction was a surge of joy and thankfulness at the doctor's good news. Immediately after which she felt weak and drained. She hadn't realized how tense or nervous she'd been till the anxiety had dissolved and her body relaxed.

After the initial relief came a wave of empathy for Casey's parents. How frightened they must have been, and how worried and tired from the trip. She wanted to rush over and hug them and share their tears of happiness.

The thought suddenly struck Paige that these people didn't even know who she was. She would appear crazy if she rushed over and hugged them. She would have to walk over calmly and introduce herself.

"Hello, I'm Paige Bannister...and I'm considering the possibilities of a relationship with your son." Or maybe, "Hello, I'm the woman who probably would have slept with your son tonight if he hadn't gotten hurt." Or how about "Hello, my name is Paige and I didn't like your son at all when I first met him, but now I've decided he's pretty special and..." And what? Oh, God, what could she say?

She considered alternatives for almost an hour. Finally a nurse came to say that Casey had been moved into a room, and the Cavanaughs rose and followed the woman out the door. They were going to see their son. Their son. The child they had loved and raised. The son they had cherished and cared for all these years.

What right had she to intrude on them in this emotional time? She was glad she hadn't introduced herself. It was clear to her now that she had no right even to be here. What was she to Casey, anyway? The Cavanaughs—and Casey himself, for that matter—probably didn't want her here at all.

She picked up her purse, determined to leave, and a heavy sadness settled in her chest. If she could just see him before she left. If she could just make contact, even if only to say goodbye. But she couldn't, she wouldn't go into his room while his parents were there.

On impulse she decided to write him a letter. She pulled her tablet and pen from her purse.

Dear Casey, I'm leaving this with the nurse because I didn't want to disturb you while you were with your parents.

My plane leaves this afternoon, and now that I know you're on your way to recovery and have the company of your parents, I...

She scribbled through the lines and flipped to a clean page.

Casey, I stayed all night and would have come in to see you, but your parents arrived and I didn't want to intrude on the family.

As you know, I was scheduled to leave this afternoon, and since I know you're on the road to recovery now, I am going to go on back to California and turn my work in.

Enclosed is my address—I would appreciate hearing from you....

Again she flipped to a new page.

Dear Casey, I was so frightened and worried. Your getting well suddenly seemed like the most important thing in the world to me. I didn't know I could feel this way about a man.

I wanted to see you so much, but I was afraid of what your parents might think. I decided the best course of action was to catch my plane and go back and finish my work. After I'm finished I could take a break and hopefully meet you somewhere—if you're recovered, of course—or fly back here if for some reason you're still in the hospital.

I can't wait to be with you again and I'll be thinking of you every day till then.

She reread the lines and felt a rush of fear. She couldn't say those things to him, even in a letter. She crumpled the page into a ball and began again.

Casey, You certainly know how to scare a person! I've never been so relieved and happy as I was when I heard the doctor say you were going to be fine.

My plane is scheduled for this afternoon, and since your parents are here to be with you, I thought I would go on back and turn in my work.

Please call me as soon as you feel well enough for a visit. And remember, we still have an unfinished evening to make up for.

Before she could change her mind again she signed her name across the bottom and folded it into thirds. She hurried out to the nurses' station and asked for an envelope. Her hands shook as she sealed it and scrawled Casey's name across the front. The nurse smiled and promised she would deliver it personally to him.

Paige's heart pounded as she pressed the one button in the elevator. She stared at the lighted floor-number panel above the doors. Four, three, two, one. The doors slid open.

She was nearly to the main hospital entrance before she remembered that her car was still at the rodeo arena. She turned back and found a pay phone to call a cab. A twenty-minute wait, they said.

She wandered through the gift shop, absently reading the magazine and paperback titles on the shelves. The hands on her watch crawled.

What would he think of the letter? Had she presumed too much when she'd written it? What if he wasn't interested in calling her or seeing her again? Had she been too forward?

She raced back up to the fifth-floor nurses' station.

"Could I have my letter back, please," she asked breathlessly.

"I've already taken it in to him," the nurse said with a puzzled expression.

"Oh," Paige breathed, and swallowed hard.

"He's awake now," the nurse said. "Why don't you go on in and see him."

Paige shook her head and muttered things about catching a plane as she backed away from the desk. Finally she turned, saw the stairs and didn't stop running until she stood on the sidewalk in front of the big old building.

# Chapter Nine

So what was the man like?" Trisha asked as they walked across the grassy knoll in Golden Gate Park.

The weak, early spring sun had given way to a chilly grayness. Paige tugged the zipper of her parka closer to her chin.

"What man?" Paige asked, almost too casually.

"The man you went to San Antonio to see."

"I don't know where you get all your ideas, Trish," Paige countered evasively. "Now what do you think, should we go ahead and do the zoo? Or maybe a museum?"

"Zoo," the girl answered. "Some more of the animals might have had their babies."

They altered course slightly to head in the direction of the huge zoo-complex entrance.

"Tell me some more about the river and the Alamo and stuff," Trisha said.

Paige smiled. She was beginning to feel like a taped travelogue.

"The river was magical," Paige began. "It was such a surprise, hidden down there below the rest of the city. It was like stepping into another world. There were little curved stone bridges and waterfalls and ornate iron benches and old-fashioned lights. We took a boat ride—"

"You and the man," Trisha cut in.

Paige sighed loudly. "All right. Yes, there was a man in San Antonio, but I met him on business. I was assigned to do some research on him for one of my company's PR campaigns."

"Likely story," the girl said sarcastically.

"Oh, Trish, stop talking like..." Paige caught herself just in time. "Like that."

"You mean like my mother," Trisha said. "I read a book that says I'm bound to grow up like her, anyway, cause she's my female role model. I mean, I'm probably pickin' up some kinda stuff from you, too, but she's my main influence."

Paige maintained a cautious silence. She would not, under any circumstances discuss the girl's mother with her. "What book did you read?" she asked finally.

The girl shrugged. "Something in school. Most of it was pretty dumb."

Paige waited, hoping the child would decide to tell her more about the contents of the book.

Trisha's look was almost one of challenge as she

spoke. "Anyway," she began, her eyes fastened on Paige's, "mom says that if you did go down there chasin' after some guy it means you're probably normal, after all."

It almost made Paige laugh. Almost, but not quite. She was afraid if she began by laughing, the laughter would turn into tears.

"Yes, your mother's right. I probably am normal," she answered with a catch in her throat.

He hadn't called. He still hadn't called. Yes, she probably was normal, after all. She felt the hurt and rejection, she felt the pain, just like anyone else would have.

"I'll race you to the tree," she challenged the girl, and ran blindly down the slope.

Casey reached down and pushed the button that raised the head of his bed. The television crackled to life. He tried another button. The entire bed started down toward the floor. He pushed button after button. The lights flickered and the radio blared, but the head of his bed remained stubbornly in place.

"Damned ignorant hunk of metal," he muttered under his breath.

He tried to turn so he could see the buttons, but the slightest movement lit a fire in his ribs.

A nurse walked in, smiling, and said cheerfully, "How's our star athlete doing this morning."

"Fine," he answered automatically. "Since you're here, you could get this damned bed to raise my head a little."

She smiled broadly and bustled into action. She

raised the bed, fluffed the pillows, smoothed the sheets and retucked them, turned off the blaring radio and television and adjusted the blinds so that bright bands of sunshine streaked the walls and floor.

"Thanks," Casey said. "It's lucky you happened along when you did. I was having a terrible argument with this bed."

"I've heard about your disagreements with the bed," she said, laughing. "And I didn't just happen along. You pushed your call button."

"Oh," he said sheepishly.

"Where are your parents today?" she asked.

"They went home last night," he said.

"I'm surprised," the nurse said. "When I talked to your mother day before yesterday, she made it pretty clear that she wasn't leaving town until you were back on your feet again."

"Yeah," Casey said, smiling. "She was a little tough to convince, but there was no sense in them staying. Nothing they could do here, and they'd been away from home long enough."

"I guess with the rodeo over all your friends have gone to wherever," she said. "I'll bet you're getting lonely and bored in here."

He would have shrugged if the action didn't cause so much pain.

"I'm used to being alone," he said. "But it is getting pretty dull. Doctor says five or six more days, but I figure I can stand about two more before I get cabin fever and have to clear out. Then somebody else can have this bed."

She laughed again. She was pretty in a robust,

healthy sort of way. Her short hair looked clean and shiny in the morning sunlight. Her eyes were almost the color of Paige's. Almost, but not quite.

"The floor won't be the same when you leave," she said in a teasing tone. "You're the hit of the nurses' station. The single gals can't wait for your call light to come on."

"Sure," he said, and caught the laugh before it made his ribs hurt.

"Yeah," she said, and sighed. "You're gonna break a lot of hearts if you leave in two days. A lotta hearts."

"Sure," he said again. "And if you keep tryin' to make me laugh, I'm reporting you for cruelty."

She chuckled to herself as she bustled back out through the swinging door.

The room settled into a bright, sunlit silence. He clicked on the television and stared at the screen as he pushed the buttons for one channel after another. Nothing caught his interest.

He closed his eyes, and the images flooded his mind. Images of Paige. She seemed to always be there on the fringes of his consciousness, as though she lived inside him now...as though she were now a part of him, inescapable and unavoidable.

He shifted in the bed and grimaced at the sharp pain movement brought. All this time in bed with little to do but think had brought on a new worry for him. How much longer did he have? Rodeo was a young man's sport, and he had been competing successfully in the riding events longer than most. How much more time did he have? How much longer till his reflexes slowed and his judgment blurred and injuries like this became common? How much longer till his body didn't heal so fast and he spent more time out of competition than in?

Rodeo was his life, his dream, his identity. He knew someday he would have to give it up. He had always known that. Few professional sports are lifetime careers. Still, knowing something intellectually and believing it emotionally are two different things.

He had never really believed it. He saw that now. He saw that he had believed himself and his abilities to be invincible, ageless, changeless. He had never really believed there would be an end.

Now suddenly the cold, hard facts were bearing down on him. He was not immortal. He was not invincible. His time as an athlete was limited. The thought was terribly painful, but he could not deny the truth of it.

And the acceptance of that truth made the few remaining years he had left take on a new importance. If his dream had to end, then it was vital that he make the most of the precious time remaining.

His thoughts shifted back to Paige. What if she didn't approve? What if she objected to his being a rodeo cowboy at all? How many times had he seen it happen—where women are attracted to professional cowboys knowing exactly what rodeo life entails when they enter into the relationship. Then, as soon as things get serious, they suddenly insist the man quit the sport.

He had never been able to understand how the guys got themselves roped into such situations. Now it was clear to him. He wanted her bad enough that he might almost consider quitting himself if she required it. Almost... but of course he could never actually go through with it, no matter how much he might want to. He couldn't throw away what was left of his dreams.

Blindly he reached out to the stand next to the bed and felt for the letter.

Casey, You certainly know how to scare a person! I've never been so relieved and happy as I was when I heard the doctor say you were going to be fine.

My plane is scheduled for this afternoon, and since your parents are here to be with you, I thought I would go on back and turn in my work.

Please call me as soon as you feel well enough for a visit. And remember, we still have an unfinished evening to make up for.

He knew the letter by heart now. He had been reading it over and over again for more than a week. And he'd intended to call her. As soon as he'd read the letter the first time he'd assumed he would call her. Didn't she say. "Please call me as soon as you feel well enough for a visit." She obviously wanted him to call her. The time just never seemed right. His parents had been there, or a doctor, or a nurse. Or else it had been too late at night, or too early in the morning, or during her working hours, when she wouldn't be home to answer, anyway. And of course he'd never call her at work.

And what if she'd changed her mind by now? What if she were no longer interested in talking to him? What if the magic she'd felt while with him in San Antonio had dissolved into disinterest. Did he dare hope for too much? Should he take the risk of allowing himself to believe she hadn't changed her mind? Doubts nagged at him, but he gritted his teeth and gingerly reached for the phone, anyway. He listened to the hollow, endless ringing for five minutes before he hung up.

Three weeks. Three unbearable weeks had passed since Paige had flown home from San Antonio. She awoke each morning in a heavy fog of depression. She plodded through the days without noticing their content. She huddled beneath her covers at night in weary hopelessness. If he hadn't called by now he never would. And she couldn't call him. Her pride wouldn't allow it. She had gone too far already with the letter. She should never have written the letter. She should never have taken the risk.

She would get over it. In time she would forget him. She kept telling herself that, but how much time would it take? How long would she dream of him at night? How long would she recall his face and his voice and his touch so clearly that it caused her to ache inside?

She muddled through her work, grateful for its utilization of her time, but only Trisha kept her from sinking completely into some dark, dismal morass. Paige looked across the Monopoly board and smiled at the expression of total concentration the girl wore as she purchased a piece of property and recounted her money.

Paige picked up the dice and rolled for her turn.

"Heard from my dad yesterday," the girl announced casually.

"You did?" Paige remarked, careful to keep her voice casual, as well.

"Yeah, he's got some kind of job and he's wanting to see mom and me."

"How do you feel about that?" Paige asked.

Trisha shrugged noncommittally. "He probably won't even show up," the girl said, running her finger back and forth across the fold in the game board.

Paige could think of nothing to say in return. The girl's words held so much. There was yearning and pain, and fear of hope, fear of disappointment. How cruel the world could be, Paige thought. "Do you want him to show up?" she finally asked.

Trisha didn't even hesitate. "Sure," she said, as though it were a given. "Maybe it won't work out again, but you never know. It might someday. Someday we might be happy together again. That's all that's important. You can't run away from stuff or quit tryin', just cause it gets scary."

*My God,* Paige thought, *here's a twelve-year-old who knows more about life than I do.*

The phone rang, breaking the stillness and causing Trisha to throw up her hands in adolescent disgust.

"It's probably mom," she groaned.

"I'll see if she won't let us finish the game," Paige promised as she rose and headed for the phone.

"Hello," she said.

"Hello, Paige...? This is Casey, Casey Cavanaugh."

She froze. Her hand felt cold clutching the receiver and her heart thudded loudly in her ears. "Yes," she managed to say.

"I've been meaning to call you," he said. "I mean, I have tried to call you, but I guess I never called at the right time, and... well... anyway... how are you?"

"Fine," she answered quickly, "just fine. How are you doing?"

"Fine. I'm fine. I'm ready to get back in shape, start ridin' again."

"Oh, that's good. I'll bet you're anxious to get back into it."

There was a brief, hesitant silence.

"I, ah, I got your letter. The nurse gave it to me."

"Oh, that... that was just, you know, I couldn't leave without saying something. I mean, your parents were there in the room with you, and so I..."

"You should have come in," he said. "If I'd known you were out there... I... well, I'd have liked them to meet you."

"I didn't want to intrude," she said, twining and untwining the phone cord between her fingers.

Unspoken questions hung on the air between them. Paige closed her eyes tightly and tilted the receiver away from herself so he couldn't hear the ragged cadence of her breathing. Her mind raced as fast as her heart. Yet she was almost afraid to hope.

"I'm heading out to Los Angeles to a rehabilitation camp for athletes," he said finally. "I've been there once before. It's a good place to get back in shape.

Anyway ... it's fairly close to you. To San Francisco. And I thought ..."

Paige held her breath and waited.

"I thought I might fly on up and say hello."

She swallowed hard and wondered if her voice would work. "That sounds fine," she said, and marveled at the even normalcy of her tone. "When will you come in?"

"Day after tomorrow," he said. "If that's all right."

"Yes, that's good for me." She was suddenly conscious of Trisha's wide staring eyes and knowing smile. She turned her back on the girl and lowered her voice self-consciously.

"I thought I'd fly into San Francisco International," he continued. "How far do you live from there?"

"I live down the peninsula in San Carlos, but that's no problem," she added quickly. "In fact, it's closer to the airport. I could pick you up any time."

"I was thinking," he said hesitantly, "I've never seen much of San Francisco. Haven't been much of any place but the rodeo grounds. And I thought you might be able to show me the sights. Unless you're tired of it ... living there and all."

"No, no," she reassured him quickly. "I actually live quite a ways out of the city, and I always enjoy spending time there. I'd love to show you around."

"Then we'll make it sort of a vacation," he said. "I'll get a couple rooms someplace right in the center of the city, and we can sightsee till we drop."

"I don't know," Paige said hesitantly. "I probably should just come back home nights."

"Sure," he said. "Whatever you feel most comfortable with. I just thought I should get a room somewhere for myself. I mean, I didn't expect to stay at your place. And if I got you a room, too, it would save you driving back and forth . . . especially late at night . . . if we stay out very late at the theater or something. Or . . . well, I just didn't know what the best thing to do would be."

"I don't know," she said, suddenly embarrassed and uncertain. She didn't want to invite him to stay with her, so the only alternative was his getting a room. And it would be better for him to stay in a nice place in the city, than in one of the dives out on the highway close to where she lived. And he was right; it was a long drive for her to have to make alone each night after doing the town in San Francisco till the wee hours.

"All right," she said, "we'll stay in the city, but I'll take care of my own room. And since I'm the one who's familiar with the city, I may as well make the reservations."

"Sure," he agreed quickly. "Whatever . . . that's fine with me."

They worked out the mechanics of time and place, and Paige hung up the phone with trembling hands. She turned and tried to act nonchalant as she took her place across the Monopoly board from Trisha.

"Was that him?" the girl asked eagerly.

"Who?" Paige asked as she straightened her piles of money and deeds.

"You know who," Trisha said. "Whoever you've been moping over the past couple of weeks."

Paige felt herself blushing.

"Was it the guy you went to San Antonio to see?" the girl went on ruthlessly. "The guy who was just business?"

Paige took a deep breath and frowned her most adult, disapproving frown. "Patricia," she said sternly.

"I know, I know," the girl said, "it's none of my business. Am I gonna get to meet him though?"

Paige couldn't help but laugh. "Maybe," she said gently. "I'm not even sure myself what's going to happen. If he comes here, to the apartment, I promise I'll introduce you to him."

The girl gave a whoop of delight and then bent back over the board, intent on winning the game. Paige studied the bent head a moment, marveling over the perceptiveness and resiliency of youth. Then she let her mind wander.

She felt light and free and warm and supremely happy. He had called—had been trying to call her for days—had been thinking about her just as she'd been thinking of him. He wanted to see her, to spend some time with her. He was coming especially to see her all the way from Los Angeles. Sure, he was going to be in California. But L.A. was still a lot of miles from San Francisco.

She played back his words in her mind. He had sounded so hesitant, so self-conscious. Could this mean as much to him as it did to her? She wanted to believe it did, but she was afraid to. Believing in and trusting a person involved so much risk. She wasn't sure she had the courage to take such a risk.

Separate rooms at a hotel in the city. The more she considered, it the better it sounded. The arrangement offered them both a neutral territory to come together in without any promises or assumptions. Separate rooms, with a door to close and lock if she chose to. And if worse came to worse she could always just get in her car and drive home.

She knew in her heart, though, that there would be no going home alone. She had another chance at happiness with Casey Cavanaugh and there was no way she was going to run away from it. As Trisha so wisely put it, "You can't run away from stuff just cause it gets scary." If she did drive home it would probably be with him, not alone.

She looked around her apartment in a sudden panic. What if she did bring him here? She had never spent much money or time on furniture and accessories. What would he think of it? Would it look dull and plain to him?

She moved her playing piece mechanically around the board and considered the possibilities within the time frame and her current checkbook balance. She passed Go and added the two hundred dollars to her stack of money. There wasn't enough time to paint the walls. Could she afford a new living-room rug? She handed Trisha the rent for Park Place with two hotels. Maybe if she moved her favorite print, the one with the brass frame, from her bedroom and hung it behind the couch. . . .

"You're not paying attention," Trisha accused her. "You should have bought that last railroad you landed on."

"I didn't see it," Paige admitted. "You're just better at this game than I am."

"No, I'm not. Not usually, anyway. You've never

let me end up with all the railroads *and* all the utilities before."

Paige laughed. "This could be your lucky day," she said as she landed on another of Trisha's vast holdings.

Plants. She would go out tomorrow and buy lots of plants. She would fill the empty corners of her apartment with plants. She loved plants, anyway, and welcomed any excuse to buy more.

And what on earth would she wear? Nothing she could think of seemed right. She would have to go through her closets and do some creative thinking.

And supposing, just supposing, she ended up spending the night in his bed. All she had for sleepwear were flannel granny gowns and oversized T-shirts. Somehow those didn't seem right for the occasion.

Paige passed the time until his arrival in a fever of anticipation. Would things be the same between them? Would they be able to pick up the threads of their tenuous relationship and go back to where they'd been before Casey's injury? She couldn't answer for him, but she knew she could. If anything, she felt she'd already gone beyond what she'd felt for him then. Her mind had been so filled with him the past weeks that she now felt a closeness, an intimacy they'd never quite reached when they were together.

That's what she believed, anyway. She believed it through all her fevered plans for his arrival. She believed it on the drive through the Bayshore Freeway's heavy traffic. She believed it right up until the time actually came and he stood in front of her in the lobby of San Francisco International Airport. She believed it—until she felt her pulse race and her hands grow cold and suddenly she wasn't so sure anymore. Suddenly she felt shy and uncertain.

There was little conversation and no touching as they walked through the crowded building and settled into her car together. She pulled into the exit lane and glanced over at him. He was paler since the accident, and somehow, in spite of the broad shoulders, he seemed almost fragile. He turned his head toward her, caught her glance and smiled. It was the same heart-stopping smile she remembered, and yet it wasn't. Something had changed. The confidence and charming boyish bravado were gone. With a shock she realized he was as frightened as she was! The knowledge restored some of her balance.

"I want you to know," she said in a perfectly serious tone, "that I'm going to try to be on my best behavior. But if at any time you should feel threatened or think I'm getting out of hand, you can always just go to your room and lock the door."

Casey's eyes widened in surprise and he stared at her as if he couldn't believe what he'd just heard.

She chuckled at his first reaction and laughed harder and harder with his continued amazement. Then he started to laugh, too, sheepishly at first, gaining confidence as the laughter built, until she knew they'd broken the barrier. Everything was going to be fine from now on.

The Four Seasons-Clift was a beautiful hotel in the grand old manner. Courtly, uniformed bellmen whisked away her car and dispatched the luggage to their individual rooms. Paige opened the connecting door wide between the rooms and quickly arranged her belongings.

She scooped up her travel guide and map and called to Casey through the doorway, "Wear your walking shoes. We'll be on foot most of the time."

The day was almost warm. It was a wonderful day, she thought, a perfect day for walking. His arm went briefly around her as he reached out to hold the door open. His fingers touched hers as she handed him the map. Union Square seemed unusually beautiful to her. Everything was wonderful. Everything was beautiful.

They strolled slowly down the wide sidewalks, weaving in and out of the bustling crowds. Suddenly Casey took her hand and pulled her to the side. He had spotted a flower cart.

She stood quietly while he discussed flower choice with the vendor. When he'd made the purchase he turned to her and held out a delicate spray of lilacs.

"They would look nice in your hair," he said.

Paige met his eyes and the look held. She could feel herself melting inside. "Yes," she said, accepting the flowers. She cupped the spray in her hand and held it up to breathe in its sweet perfume. Her eyes met his again, and she felt almost weak under his dark, warm gaze.

She was trembling as she fastened the flowers into her hair. He reached up to help her, and his hands were warm and steady on hers. It seemed only natural that the contact should continue, and they held hands as they moved off down the street.

"Where would you like to go first?" she asked him.

"How about Fisherman's Wharf," he said. "We could have lunch there, too."

They found the cable-car stop and waited. Paige stared off into the distance, at a loss for conversation. Her hand felt warm in his. She had so much she wanted to say to him, but she wasn't ready yet. She couldn't say the words out loud yet.

They walked along the pier and watched the fishing boats. They feasted on crab and shrimp and sourdough bread thick with butter. They browsed through Ghiradelli Square and laughed their way through the Ripley's Believe It Or Not Museum.

They talked, but the conversation was safe and light. High school and college and family and remembered pets. The more they talked, the more eager Paige grew. She wanted to hear everything about him. She wanted to know all there was to know and more. And she searched for clues in his words. How did he feel about her? What was he thinking? Did he know how she felt?

The light softened into dusk, and a cool breeze stirred off the ocean. She shivered, and he circled her shoulders with his arm and drew her close to the warmth of his body. She closed her eyes and drank in the closeness of him, the textures of his clothes and skin and hair and the clean masculine smell of him. She wanted to stand there like that on the sidewalk of Fisherman's Wharf forever.

They caught the cable car back and climbed the hill away from the ocean. Lights twinkled below them, and she could see the tiny flashing caution lights on the bridges in the distance. She settled closer to him on the bench in the darkness and listened to the rattle of the car beneath her. The night wind blew against her cheeks and she could smell the ocean.

He reached up to touch her cheek and she turned toward him. The kiss was mutual. He pulled her closer into the circle of his arms, and she laid her head on his shoulder and closed her eyes. It was a moment frozen in time. A moment she knew she'd remember in detail for the rest of her life.

The restaurant they chose for dinner was called Mama Louisa's. It was charmingly quaint and romantic and highly recommended as having the best home-made pasta in all of San Francisco.

They were seated at a small round table in a dark corner. Candlelight danced on the walls and cast a golden glow on their faces.

Mama Louisa herself came to take their order. "You hungry tonight?" she asked them, rings sparkling on her chubby fingers.

They nodded and laughed.

"I got lotsa good things tonight," she said. "Four kinds of fresh fish and six pastas and good veal and plenty of chicken. I got whatever you're hungry for."

Casey folded his menu and handed it to the woman. "We'll leave it up to you," he said with a grin. "Bring us the best you've got."

The woman chuckled and winked at him. "And how about the wine," she said. "This table needs a wonderful bottle of red wine."

"Again your choice," Casey told her. "But please make it special."

The chuckle rumbled inside her again, and she

reached out to briefly pat their shoulders. "I like the lovers," she said. "I always take the lovers' orders. You lovers make me feel good, like when I was young." She chuckled again and disappeared.

They laughed together and their hands met across the white tablecloth. Their eyes touched and held.

"She thought we were lovers," Casey said and his voice and his eyes asked the question, "Are we?"

The wine was poured, and Casey raised his glass in a silent toast. Candlelight sparkled on the etched crystal and reflected in the dark ruby of the wine and the dark blue of his eyes.

Paige felt herself falling, falling into some heady, unknown realm from which there was no return. She raised her glass to his.

"To lovers," she said and her voice held the answer.

She ate when the fragrant, steaming platters of food came and she drank the rich, red wine, but the meal was lost on her. She barely was conscious of her actions. Her senses were too filled with him and the anticipation of being in his arms.

*Lovers.* The word echoed through her mind all the way back to the hotel.

## Chapter Ten

He unlocked the door to his room and she stepped inside without question. They settled on the couch together, talking about small things—the dinner, the day, the colors of the room. He pulled her close as they talked, and Paige settled easily against him, his arm around her and her head on his shoulder.

He kissed her forehead first, then tilted her chin up and kissed her lips. The kiss was gentle and tender. Her heart raced in her chest and she questioned her decision to be there. Was this right? Was this what she really wanted? Always the answers were yes.

He reached up and pulled the flowers from her hair. Slowly, carefully, he pulled the pins out of her chignon until the heavy weight of curls cascaded down around her shoulders and face. He brushed it back from her forehead and buried his face in it, breathing deeply.

"I love the way your hair smells," he said.

"This is not a game for me," she said suddenly, realizing the time for talking was quickly running out.

"I know," he said. "I know. It's not a game for either of us."

He kissed her again. His lips were soft at first, then gradually more insistent. He leaned back against the arm of the couch and pulled her close to him. Her breathing grew fluttery and uneven. He kissed her and pulled her tighter and tighter against him, until she felt the heat where her soft breasts and belly and thighs met his hard leanness. She felt as if she were melting inside.

The kissing was constant now. There were no beginnings and no endings, just a continuous flowing need. She ran her fingers through his thick, wavy hair and down his neck and touched the rippling muscles of his back. She couldn't touch him enough. She wanted to know the feel of every angle and texture of him.

Her breathing quickened, and she felt herself losing track of time and place. She was spiraling downward into some infinite, timeless state where all that mattered was this man and the sharp electric pleasures his hands brought as they traveled over her body and cupped her breasts through the silk of her dress.

Slowly he undid her buttons and traced the shape of her nipples with his fingers. She quivered at the delightful feel of his callused hands against the smoothness of her bare skin. His mouth traveled down her throat, and she leaned her head back and closed her eyes and wove her fingers into his hair. His lips trailed fire across her skin, and she moaned softly when his tongue found her nipple.

He caressed her with his mouth and hand, until she felt a desperate heat in her loins, a surging need to possess and be possessed by him. She was barely conscious of being lifted and carried to the wide bed....

Passions spent, they lay quietly for a time. A tear escaped and ran down her cheek. She brushed it away quickly, afraid he might misunderstand. It was a tear of joy, of wonder, of reverence.

He buried his head in the curve of her neck and murmured her name softly. A wave of love and tenderness swept over her, and more tears slipped from her eyes.

"Are you crying?"

"No...yes. Just a little."

"You're sorry," he said.

"No! I'm just so...so happy."

He brushed the tears from her face with his fingers and then looked into her eyes. His loving gaze filled her with warmth.

"I love you," she said, and the words hung in the air between them. She realized now that she'd said it before without realizing what the phrase even meant. Without the words or the emotions being real.

"Oh, God," he moaned, laying his head on her breast. "I love you, too. Never knew anything could be like this."

"Me, too," she said. "I never imagined I could feel

so much love . . . so much passion. There's so much I want you to know, so many things I want to tell you, but it's so hard to put it all into words.''

"Don't even try," he said, and kissed her gently. "Just sleep. We'll worry about words tomorrow."

She spent the night snuggled tightly beside him in his bed, and never once thought of her own room or of locking doors or of going home.

Casey propped himself up on one elbow and watched her sleep. The drapes were closed, but enough morning sun crept in to allow him to see her. She was so beautiful. He traced the planes of her face and the curve of her neck and the sensuous swell of her breasts with his eyes.

He loved her. The thought came to him in such a natural, easy manner that he almost missed its presence. When he fully grasped the significance he was staggered. Love? He said it last night, but somehow it was far more significant in the light of morning. He'd never loved a woman before. Wanted them, yes. Had fun with them, yes. Made love, yes. But to actually be in love. The thought almost panicked him.

What did it all mean? Visions of houses and yards and two-car garages filled his mind. Marriage. How else could he possibly hold on to her? How else could he possibly spend the rest of his life with her? But marriage didn't go with professional rodeo. It was usually an either-or situation. Wives didn't often put up with the profession of rodeo as their husband's occupation. Too much danger. Too much risk. Too much travel. Too much uncertainty.

He'd seen it happen so many times. A guy would bring his girlfriend around, and she would be talking about buying a house somewhere and settling down, and they would get married. And before you knew it the guy wasn't on the circuit anymore, or there was a divorce.

All he had ever wanted to be was a cowboy. His whole life had been tied into that dream. Could he give up the years he had left for her? Could he settle down in some town and put on a tie and work from nine to five?

Maybe she wouldn't want that from him. Maybe she would be one of those rare women who could happily share the rodeo life. He certainly wouldn't ask her to give up her career or any portion of her existence that meant anything to her. Maybe, just maybe it could work. If it didn't, how could he go on? He didn't want to live without her. Yet how could he be whole without his dream?

She stirred, and he reached over to brush a strand of hair from her cheek. She opened her eyes and smiled at him. It was a lazy, slow smile. A contented smile. It did crazy things to his heart.

"How long have you been awake?" she asked, reaching up to touch his hair lightly with her fingertips.

"Not long," he said.

"Were you watching me?"

"Yes, do you mind?"

"I don't look too good in the morning," she said. "Couldn't you wait till I'd combed my hair and brushed my teeth before you looked?"

"You look beautiful to me," he said, grinning.

"And hungry," she said. "I could eat a farmhand's meal."

He reached behind him for the phone and dialed room service. "Breakfast in twenty minutes," he said. "We have time for a shower first."

"Go ahead," she said, stretching her arms out over her head. "I'm still too comfortable."

He stood under the running water of the shower and let the hard, hot spray hit his back and shoulders. He couldn't just ask her. Not yet. After all, how would he say it? They hadn't even vaguely discussed marriage. He was only assuming she'd be interested. He could just hear himself saying, "There's something we should settle now before we both get too much deeper in this.... What if we thought there was a chance we might want to get married... how would you feel about my rodeo career? How would you feel about a husband who traveled a lot and voluntarily risked his neck on a daily basis. Could you live with that?" He couldn't possibly say that.

Why was it, he wondered as he mechanically worked the soap into a lather, that the most important questions in people's lives were the ones they couldn't ask.

Paige couldn't remember ever being so happy. She stood beside him at Coit Tower and the Golden Gate Bridge and on Lombard Street and thought of nothing but how happy she was... how much she loved him.

She walked the streets of Chinatown holding his hand, and she ate Chinese food looking into his eyes. "Someone important will come into your life," her fortune said, and she laughed with him till she had tears in her eyes.

They used every excuse to touch, to be close. Everything seemed glowing and funny and warm. She wondered why she'd been so frightened of love. Love was wonderful. She wanted to announce it to the world. She wanted to shout it out loud.

When she saw the fountain she didn't even hesitate. She ran to the blue-tiled circle and pulled off her shoes.

"What are you doing?" Casey called from behind her.

"The fountain," she said. "It's just the right fountain."

And it was. It was a perfect fountain. Classically symmetrical. Just the kind of fountain she had always imagined Zelda in.

Casey caught up to her just as she stepped over the edge and into the chilly water. "Hey, wait a minute! It's too cold for that," he said, and reached out to grab her arm.

When his hand touched her she turned and lost her balance on the slick tile. Her feet flew out from under her, and she fell with a splash into the icy water. Sputtering and gasping, she hit the tiles with her bottom and settled into a sitting position in the chest-deep water.

"Paige!" she heard Casey cry, and she wiped the water from her eyes in time to see him jumping over the edge, cowboy boots and all.

He floundered through the water, bent to slide his hands under her arms and lifted her several inches, before the slick leather of his boot soles began to slide. He dropped her, arms and legs flailing for balance, but this was no bull. His hat flew off and he splashed down beside her with a yell.

Paige started to giggle. This wasn't how Zelda did it. She'd never be Zelda. She'd never be Judy. But somehow that didn't matter anymore.

She threw dripping arms around his neck and kissed him wildly.

"Hey," Casey said, laughing now between the wet kisses.

He stood up, pulling her to her feet with him, and together they slipped and slid to the edge and stepped out. "You're crazy!" he said, and grinned that wonderful grin she loved.

"I think one fountain in my life will be enough," she said, shivering.

"One fountain and one man," he said, pulling her into his arms.

She leaned against him, lost in his warmth, completely and totally happy in the secure haven of his arms. He kissed her tenderly, and the world dissolved into nothingness around her.

"Hey!" he suddenly cried. "My hat!"

She turned to see his waterlogged hat sinking slowly. She raced to the edge beside him, and together they fished the soggy lump from the water.

With a wistful look he straightened and slowly tipped the hat over, spilling water onto the concrete walk.

"It's not ten gallons," she said, trying to suppress a grin,

"Very funny," he said. "Very funny."

He jammed the shapeless wet hat down on his head and challenged her with a playful scowl.

"Great," she assured him. There was no controlling the grin now. "Looks just great. You ought to wear them shaped like that all the time."

"Yeah, well, next time warn me when you feel like a swim," he said. "So I can at least take a few things off."

"I promise," she said.

"Now come on," he said slipping his arm around her waist. "Let's get some dry clothes on before we freeze."

They spent the rest of the afternoon at the Japanese Tea Garden and the de Young Museum. Her mind whirled with joyous plans. She would take him home and introduce him to everyone she knew. She would cook him dinner. She would have Trisha over and they would all play games or pop corn or listen to music. Trisha would be crazy about him. And then maybe they would talk about the future, about their future together.

She could hardly sit through dinner. She could hardly eat. She could think of nothing but Casey. She could see and hear and feel nothing but Casey. She felt as though she could exist the rest of her life with nothing for sustenance but him.

When they returned to his room that night there was no hesitation and no pretense. He slipped off her clothing and she helped him with his. He kissed her long and hard, and the world reeled about her. Through heavy lashes she watched him bend over her, watched the hard, taut leanness of his body, and she thought she might die of wanting him.

"I love you," she whispered as he enveloped her with his hands and his mouth and his body.

She was caught in a vortex, spinning, falling, being carried away from herself and reality. Reality was Casey's body pressed against hers. Reality was the aching need inside her.

"I love you," Casey said when their lovemaking was over and they were nestled close together on the big bed.

The thought, and the words, came easily to him now. He couldn't remember saying anything in his life that felt so right.

She kissed the bare skin of his chest lightly.

"Not as much as I love you," she said.

"What makes you say that?" he asked, smiling to himself in the dark.

"You just couldn't," she said playfully. "No one could love anyone as much as I love you."

He laughed and lifted her hand to his mouth to kiss the palm.

"How do I prove how much?" he asked, still in the playful spirit of the exchange.

"Come home with me tomorrow morning," she said, and her tone was suddenly serious. "Meet the people I work with, spend some time with Trisha. Watch television with me and cook dinner with me and spend the night in my bed."

Somewhere in the back of his mind a warning flashed.

"That sounds like an easy enough way to prove something," he said, wondering if he was right.

"You will? You really will!" she cried.

Her excitement was touching. He listened to her talk, making plans, explaining things, with quick, silvery little bursts of laughter in between. She was like a child delighted by some prospective visit to an amusement park.

"I'll take you by all the points of interest in San Carlos," she said. "There must be at least one. And I'll take you to my favorite restaurant for lunch. They have terrific seafood and chocolate mousse for dessert and the best fresh vegetables you've ever had. Good hand-cut French fries, too, but I try to stay away from those. Too fattening."

"But the chocolate mousse isn't?" he asked innocently.

"Well, the mousse is dessert," she insisted. "Desserts are supposed to be fattening. You're allowed to feel guilty about desserts."

"The whole place sounds fattening to me," he said, "but, then, I don't ever really worry about what I eat. I guess I burn it all off riding and jogging."

"Disgusting," she said, and giggled gleefully.

"We'll go by work," she continued in a breathless rush. "And I'll show you my office and introduce you to Maggie Carson, my boss, and all the other people on my floor, and I'll show you the water cooler and other important points."

She twisted free of his arm and propped herself up on her elbow. He could just make out her outline in the darkened room.

"Let's see," she went on, "I could introduce you to my landlady and take you by the grocery store where I shop and..."

"I'm not *that* interesting," he said with a laugh.

"That's what you think," she teased, and reached over to playfully slap his arm.

"And tomorrow evening sometime I'd like to call Judy and Ken and tell them how happy we are. Maybe we could find out where they're going to be traveling together and the four of us could meet and have a wonderful time. Won't they be surprised when we call?"

"Yes," Casey said. "Ken won't believe it."

And he knew why Ken wouldn't believe it. Ken wouldn't believe that Casey would give up rodeo for a woman, and Ken would automatically assume that that's what had to happen for Casey and Paige ever to be happy together. He had heard Ken talk about the subject before. Had heard him talk about how it was next to impossible to be married and to rodeo... how it took a very special woman to cope with it all, and how lucky he had been to find Judy, who was indeed a very special woman.

Again and again he had heard Ken discuss all the divorces, all the failed relationships. "It's so seldom anybody's fault," he always said, "It's just a damn hard life."

"My apartment isn't anything very special," she was saying. "I mean it's just an apartment. It doesn't have the coziness of a house, and of course there's no yard or any place for pets. I don't care what a person does to them—apartments just never have that settled, permanent feeling. I never have been able to get very excited about fixing mine up."

Her words caused a vague uneasiness in the back of his mind, and again he was conscious of a warning flashing somewhere.

"You'll love Trisha. She's a great kid. I'd like to have one just like her. Her problems are all due to her home life. You know, the typical story—father who ran around all the time, chasing after all kinds of crazy schemes, and wouldn't stay at home. Made life rough for his wife and child."

"Maybe he had a good reason," Casey said. "Maybe he had things to do that were important to him."

"What could be more important than your home and family?" Paige insisted.

"Maybe not more important, but . . . equally important. Dreams can be equally important."

"No," Paige said, shaking her head. "Marriage means becoming an adult, accepting the adult world. People like Trisha's father are still holding on to childish dreams. People like him who can't settle down and assume the responsibilities of parenthood and marriage shouldn't be allowed to get married. There are no excuses for them. They end up ruining too many innocent lives."

Her words burned into his brain. He didn't need to ask anymore. Her words left no room for question. He knew now what she would think of being married to a rodeo cowboy, to a man who was chasing a dream. He knew what she would think of a life with him. There was no hope, no chance to win her unless he was willing to give up his dreams.

"Are you asleep?" she whispered.

He couldn't answer her. After a while her breathing grew regular and even, and he knew she'd fallen asleep. He wrestled with the questions in his mind for hours, but there were no answers. How could he give her up, now that he had found her? On the other hand, what kind of man would he be if he gave up his career and his identity and his dreams? There would be nothing left of himself if he did that, nothing left to offer her.

Paige awoke the next morning feeling delicious, and turned lazily toward Casey in the big bed. Eyes still closed, savoring the moment, she reached for him. Her hand met only emptiness. She sat bolt upright, her eyes wide open, her senses jarred into wakefulness. The room was still and quiet.

"Casey?" she called, but the bathroom was open and dark, and she could sense the emptiness of the room. Her voice sounded hollow and unreal.

She ran to the window and opened the draperies wide. Pure morning light flooded the room and made her blink. She moved slowly back across the carpet and sat down on the edge of the bed. Nothing to worry about. He had probably gone down for coffee or a paper or something.

She opened the connecting door to her unused room and called his name again just in case, but of course there was no reason for him to be in there. She pulled on her robe and brushed her hair back from her face. It made her feel almost sad to wake up without him. She chided herself for being silly, and stepped into the small bathroom to take her shower. That's when it hit her.

His belongings were gone. Frantically she rushed from the bathroom and looked around the room. There was no sign he'd ever been there. His wallet was gone from the dresser. His clothes were missing from the closet. His boots were gone from their place beside the chair. His hat was gone from the shelf. Everything of his was gone. It was as if he'd never existed in this room.

She sank into a chair, clutching her arms tightly to her chest. Something terrible was happening. Something she didn't understand was happening. No. No. There had to be an answer. There had to be a reason. There had to be some sensible explanation for all this that would make her laugh when she heard it.

She reached for the phone as though reaching for a lifeline.

"Good morning, front desk," a male voice answered.

"Yes, could you please page a Mr. Cavanaugh," she said uncertainly, "a Mr. Casey Cavanaugh."

"I'm sorry," the voice said in a professionally courteous manner. "Mr. Cavanaugh is already gone. I checked him out myself and saw him get into a taxi. Let me see . . . he paid for two rooms and advised that one would still be occupied until checkout time. And . . . if I remember correctly . . . yes . . . he did leave a letter here. . . ." There were shuffling sounds. "If you could wait one moment please."

Paige held her breath in the silence.

"Could I have your name, please?" the voice asked.

"Bannister, Paige Bannister."

"Yes, he left a letter here for you, Miss Bannister. Shall I have it sent up?"

"Yes, please," Paige said, and swallowed hard as she hung up the phone.

There still could be a good reason. He had had an emergency call and had to rush off, and he didn't want to wake her. He had had a sudden yearning to see his parents, or he'd had a flash of ESP and rushed off to help some friend in distress. He had remembered something or someone. He had... Oh, God, please let there be a reason.

The bellman took forever to arrive. Paige accepted the envelope from him and handed him a tip. As she closed and locked the door she grew suddenly fearful and hesitant. Her hands felt cold and her heart thudded dully in her chest. She didn't want to open it. She didn't want to know. If she didn't open it she could pretend everything was all right.

The envelope was hotel stationery. Her name was printed very simply across the front. She turned it over and looked at the seal. She found herself crazily wishing for a letter opener so she could slit it neatly open and preserve it. She'd never had a letter from Casey before. This might be the only letter she ever received from Casey. She had to treat it with care.

Her hands trembled as she tore the glue loose and opened the flap. There were several pages filled with an easy, loose script. Again it was hotel stationery.

She unfolded the pages carefully and sat down on the bed to read.

Dear Paige, I don't write many letters and I'm not very good at it, but I owe you an explanation, and so I'm going to try to do my best.

I never thought I'd meet anyone like you in my life. I never made any plans or figured out what I would do if it happened, because I just never thought it would. I've been married to rodeo and I guess I thought I always would be.

Now that it has happened, I see that it can never work out. Our lives are too different. Our goals are too different. We could never make a life together, and I think it's better to face that and end everything now before this goes any further. Drawing it out will only make the pain worse.

I know most of this is my fault. I'm the one who kept after you and couldn't leave you alone. I'm the one who caused it all to happen. I know you'll probably hate me now, but I had to be honest with you as soon as I knew, and not let you go on believing a lie.

I'm sorry I didn't have the decency or the courage to wake you up and tell you this to your face. But I just couldn't bear to see you hurt, so I'm taking the coward's way out.

Please believe it when I say you're the most wonderful person I've ever met in my life, and I could never love anyone else the way I love you.
Casey.

She reread the letter twice before she let it slip from her fingers to the floor. She stared out into nothingness, numb and unaware. Words tumbled around in her mind, but nothing made sense.

She didn't know when the tears started. They were just there. And then suddenly she felt intense, physical pain, and she doubled over with the ache and buried her face in her hands and cried out into the silence.

It was hours before she could dress and gather her belongings. She moved slowly, as if in some trance, and she had trouble concentrating on what she was doing. She walked to the bathroom for her toothbrush and forgot why she had gone there. She looked into the mirror at her swollen red eyes and saw herself as a stranger.

"What did I do wrong?" she asked the red-eyed reflection. "What did I do wrong?"

She folded the silk dress and thought of his hands touching her. She walked past the bed and saw the depression still remaining on his side of the bed and the indention of his pillow. The sight was so devastating that she collapsed again into dry, racking sobs.

She lay down where he had slept and buried her face in his pillow. It still smelled like him. She could almost feel the shape and warmth of his body.

"Casey, Casey," she cried into the softness of the pillow.

She drove home mechanically, not seeing signs or landmarks at all, and she was almost surprised when she finally pulled up in front of her apartment. How had she gotten home so quickly? She sat there in her car, staring at the door and not wanting to move or go in. She knew how unbearably empty the apartment would seem now. What did she have in those rooms that mattered to her? What did she have in her life without him?

Her world had seemed entirely adequate before she met him, but now, now it seemed sterile and bleak, now it seemed like an unending series of gray days stretching on into time before her. God, how could she go through the days knowing she'd never see him or talk with him or look into the dark intensity of his eyes again?

She looked down at the letter lying on the seat beside her.

Please believe it when I say you're the most wonderful person I've ever met in my life, and I could never love anyone else the way I love you.

She couldn't read the signature, because the tears had started again.

## Chapter Eleven

Hello, Miss Bannister?"

"Yes," Paige answered.

"This is Marilyn Green, Trisha's mother."

"Yes. Hello, how are you?"

"I'm fine. I was, ah, wondering if I could come over and talk to you in a little while. If you're not busy or anything...."

"No, I'm not busy," Paige assured her. "There's nothing wrong with Trisha, is there?"

"Oh, no. Nothing like that."

"Well, then, come over anytime," Paige told her. "I don't have any plans."

She hung up the phone and almost laughed out loud. What an understatement. She didn't have any plans. She not only didn't have any plans for this afternoon or this evening, she didn't have any plans for tomorrow or next week or next year. She felt completely lost and without purpose. Nothing interested her. Nothing seemed important. Even Trisha's visits left her feeling blue.

Dutifully she moved about the apartment, straightening, dusting, mechanically getting ready for her visitor. What could the woman want? She barely had the energy to care.

Paige answered the door when the bell rang, and there stood Marilyn Green, dressed in her best, a cigarette hanging loosely out of the corner of her mouth. All Paige could seem to think of was that she didn't have an ashtray in the place.

"Can I come in?" the woman asked.

"Certainly," Paige said quickly, and stood aside.

She shut the door and turned to watch as the woman strolled about, inspecting the apartment.

"Trisha really likes it over here," the woman said as she ran her finger along the spines of the paperbacks on the bookshelf.

"She seems to enjoy herself," Paige agreed.

The woman stopped suddenly, holding her cigarette out with one hand and cupping the other hand beneath it to catch the falling clump of ash.

"Got an ashtray?"

Paige pulled the saucer from under a potted plant and handed it to the woman. The ashes were knocked off into the saucer, and then the woman settled herself into a chair. Paige followed suit, sitting across from her.

"You've been good to my Trisha."

"Well...I..." Paige faltered.

"No," Marilyn Green said, holding up a work-worn hand. "Don't bother arguin' about it. It's true, and everybody knows it. That ain't why I came." The woman hesitated, as though uncertain as to her choice of words.

"I came to tell you that we're movin' away, that we won't be livin' in California no more."

"What?" Paige said dumbly.

"We're movin'. My husband's started a new life out in Arizona. He's tryin' real hard and got a good responsible job. He wants us back."

"And you're going?" Paige cried. "You're going to drag Trisha all the way to Arizona at the drop of a hat?"

"You're damned right," the woman shot back at her. "I love that man, and if he's gonna try to settle down, then I got the guts to at least meet him half-way. We got another chance to be together. Another chance to be happy together and be a family. I know it's a risk, but ain't everything. Everything worth havin', anyways. Why should I go on bein' miserable and lonely if there's any chance of bein' happy with him?"

Paige leaned her head back against her chair and closed her eyes. Trisha leaving. God, was her entire world going to crumble away into tinier and tinier bits until there was nothing left?

She straightened and drew in a deep breath. "Does Trisha know you're here?" she asked.

The woman nodded.

"She's the one insisted I come tell you," she said.

"Told me she just couldn't tell you herself. She's pretty broke up about leavin' you."

Paige tried to swallow the lump forming in her throat.

The woman fished in her purse for another cigarette and went through the motions of lighting it.

"Fact is, Trisha's pretty worried about leavin' you. Says she's all you've got and that you're sad all the time when you're without her." The woman shrugged. "You know what strange notions kids get sometimes. She makes it sound like she's the one got you for an assignment 'stead of the other way around. She says you're too fragile and if she leaves you now you're just gonna sit in this apartment and wither away or something. Anyways," the woman said with a sigh, "I was hopin' that if I explained the whole thing to you maybe you could talk to her, convince her that you're gonna be okay without her. Would you do that?"

"Yes, of course," Paige said. "I'll try to do that, and I'm glad you explained."

She took Trisha down the coast for a picnic. The day turned out breezy and slightly chilly, but that didn't seem to matter. The ocean was a bright blue-green studded with foaming white caps. The sand sparkled clean and pale and was warm beneath their bare feet. They carried the ice chest and tote bag from the car and settled in beside a stunted cedar to eat.

"You know, Trish, I've been thinking about moving to a new place. A house, maybe. I'm making enough money now to afford it. Someplace where I could maybe have a dog for company. I've always wanted a dog."

The girl was silent.

"What do you think?"

The girl shrugged. "Dogs are okay," she said around a bite of sandwich, "but there's nothin' wrong with the place you've got now. What do you want to move for?"

"I thought it might be good for me," Paige said. "You know, change of scene and all."

Again the girl shrugged.

"I don't want you to be worried about me," Paige said finally.

The girl looked startled.

"What'd my mother tell you?" she demanded. "Never mind. If I know her she told you everything. What a big mouth she has."

"I'm glad she told me," Paige said. "I want to talk to you about it. I want you to know that you don't have to be worried about me."

"So you're gonna move and get a dog and everything's going to be fine. Don't sound so fine to me."

"You don't understand, Trish. All of us are different. I don't need the same things as some other people do. I like being by myself."

"Sure. That's why you folded up so bad when that guy took off. You like to think you're different, but you're not. You're just like my mom. You need somebody just like my mom. Only difference is you aren't tough enough to fight for it like she is."

The girl started to cry, and Paige reached out and

pulled her close. She knelt there in the sand, hugging the thin, gangly little body to her with tears of her own spilling down her cheeks.

"If you could just learn to fight like my mom, then I wouldn't be so worried about leaving," the girl sobbed. "Who's gonna take care of you and cheer you up when I'm gone?"

They held each other and cried for several minutes. There was no answer to Trisha's question.

Casey picked himself up out of the dirt, dusted off his hat and started back toward the chutes. He'd eaten a lot of dirt lately. The dirt of the Houston Astrodome tasted no different from any other.

He picked up his gear and started toward the exit.

"Say, Case, wait up," a voice called from behind him.

He knew without looking that it was Ken. He'd been trying to avoid his friend all night. Now he'd finally been caught. He stood and waited with his gear bag slung over his shoulder as Ken walked up the concrete ramp toward him.

"Been tryin' to find you all night," Ken said. "How 'bout a beer or something?"

"Isn't Judy here with you?"

"She's tired. Stayed at the room tonight to lie around a little. We didn't get here till real late last night."

"I don't know about going anywhere, Ken. I'm pretty tired myself."

"Okay. I'll just walk you to your car, then," Ken said.

Casey turned and started out of the building without comment.The night air was slightly cool and very damp. They walked past the enormous roaring unit that conditioned the Astrodome's air and then out into the quiet of the immense parking area.

"Have you stayed aboard anything since you were hurt?" Ken finally asked.

"No," Casey answered.

The moment he'd dreaded was here. He knew Ken was going to demand some answers.

"Weren't you ready to ride? Didn't you let yourself mend good enough?"

"I was ready," Casey said.

"Well, what is it, then?"

"Guess I'm just on a cold streak."

"Cold streak, hell. You haven't bucked off this many times in the whole rest of your career put together."

"It happens," Casey said. "Maybe I'm just getting too old for this."

"Old! Is that what all this is about? Have you developed some damned mental block about your age? You're only thirty. That's not young in the riding events, but it's not retirement age, either."

Casey said nothing.

"Is that it? Is it some kind of an age crisis?"

Still Casey said nothing.

"Talk to me, Case. Dammit, we go back a long ways, and you've nursed me through some rough times. You ought to have enough faith or trust or whatever in me to let me help you when you need it."

Casey drew in a deep breath. They'd reached his rental car, and he threw down his gear beside it. "It's Paige," he said finally. "I spent some time with her. We got...serious."

"What happened?"

"I finally realized the whole thing came down to a choice between her and my rodeo career. I didn't think I could give up rodeo...so I bailed out."

There was an uncomfortable silence between the two men. They weren't accustomed to discussing their emotions, and neither one found the words easy.

"Sometimes a guy has to make choices..." Ken said lamely.

"Yeah, but was it the right one? Without her rodeo doesn't seem so important anymore. I can't seem to think about anything but her."

"Did you talk to her about it? About maybe working something out?" Ken asked.

Casey shook his head. "No. Didn't seem to be much point. I could tell by the way she talked what her answers would be. Can't blame her, either. Most women feel the same way."

"You shoulda tried to talk about it. At least give her a chance to say what she thought," Ken insisted. "Sometimes women can surprise you."

"Maybe," Casey said.

"Talk to her," Ken said. "Tell her everything, and see what she says. You've got to do something. If you go on like this you might as well quit rodeo, anyway."

"I can't talk to her now. Not after I ran out on her like that. I'm sure she hates me now."

"Talk fast," Ken said. "Start explaining right off. You'll think of a way. Women always love you, Case."

"I don't know if I can."

"Hell, what are you so scared of! If she means that much to you, then get in there and try. Try just as hard as if you were going for the world. Use a little of that courage of yours just like you were getting down on a bad bull."

Casey laughed halfheartedly. Talk to her. Find out if she hated him. Find out if she was hurt and angry. And even if he managed to get beyond that point, then what? What if she still cared? What if she was still willing to make a go of it? Then he had to deal with how she felt about a relationship with a rodeo cowboy. What if she loved him and wanted him but insisted that he quit? What would he do then? How could he possibly choose?

Talk to her. It sounded so simple, but it was going to take more out of him than any ride he'd ever made. He wondered if he possessed that much courage.

Paige sat at her tiny kitchen table, looking out the window. A cold toaster waffle sat untouched in front of her. The fog was bad again today, and she wondered if it would burn off in the afternoon. Maybe it would be gray and foggy forever. Right now she felt that was a distinct possibility.

She stared down at her breakfast without seeing it. She could picture him so clearly. He was always on the fringes of her thoughts, waiting to haunt her. Would she ever be free of him? Would she ever have a night without dreams of him, without waking filled with wanting him, in the darkness of the night? Would she ever have a morning where his name was not the first thing in her thoughts as she roused?

She glanced at her watch. Not really time to leave for work yet, but there was no reason not to. She picked up a heavy sweater and her purse. The phone rang shrilly in the stillness, and she jumped.

"Hello," she said, wondering who on earth would be calling at this time of the morning.

"Paige, this is Judy. How are you?"

"Oh, hi. I'm ... well ... I'm just leaving for work."

"Well, I'd better not talk too long, then. I just wanted to tell you I saw Casey here at Houston."

"Oh," Paige said. Her heart hammered dully in her chest.

"He's not doing too well. He's ... well, he's pretty broken up over you. I've never seen him like this."

Paige laughed hollowly. "So he's broken up, is he. Am I supposed to feel sorry for him?"

"I just thought—" Judy hesitated. "I thought you might want to know."

"Why are you telling me this?"

"Because I care—about both of you," Judy said softly.

"All right. I know you mean well and I don't want to hurt your feelings, but I don't want to hear anymore. He's the one who walked out. He's the one who said goodbye. I can't help it if he's feeling bad or got a guilty conscience or whatever."

"But it's not a guilty conscience. It's ... well, he talked to Ken last night, and from what I could pry out of my husband it sounds like Casey has the idea that he has to choose between you and rodeo."

"What?" Paige asked.

"He's tearing himself apart over it, over making a choice. And I can understand why you want him to quit... but do you know what you're doing to him?"

"No!" Paige cried. "I didn't tell him that. We never even discussed the subject."

"Then how did he get that idea?" Judy asked.

"God, I don't know. Everything was fine and he just left. He just wrote me a letter and disappeared."

"Something had to have happened," Judy insisted. "Casey doesn't just imagine things. Think back. Was there anything you said?"

Paige searched back through her memory. The evening had gone so well. She was positive there'd been nothing wrong between them when they'd made love. What had she said afterward? She'd been talking about taking him home with her. About introducing him to people. About Trisha. About Trisha's father.

Slowly the realization dawned on her. She'd been talking about Trisha's father running around, chasing after schemes, and Casey had tried to defend the man. She remembered carrying on about people with childish dreams and marriage meaning settling down and learning to accept adult responsibility. And she remembered how quiet Casey had gotten.

She knew now what she had done. She knew what she had said. She knew how he had interpreted her words.

"I think I know," she said slowly. "I think I understand now."

"Well," Judy said, "I don't want to meddle or to betray any confidences, but darn it, somebody had to do something! The way this has been going you two were never going to resolve anything...and... well...I thought you should know what's going on in that stubborn man's head. I was worried he'd never tell you himself."

"What now?" Paige asked miserably. "I don't even know how to get in touch with him. I don't know what to do. I need to talk to him, but I don't know how or what or where. Do you think he'd see me, talk to me?"

"I'm positive," Judy said. "And, well, personally think Casey's worth whatever you have to go through. I'd go to him and just tell him exactly how I felt."

"I don't know if I can. I mean, I don't even know myself exactly how I feel, and I...I don't know if I can just, well, just go to him. Maybe if I just called him..."

"It's your decision," Judy said. "He's leaving for the big Las Vegas match today. He usually stays at the King Midas."

Paige couldn't speak. Her mind was racing too fast.

"I just wanted you to know everything. I better let you get to work now."

"Yes, well, I'm glad you called Judy. I know you did it out of friendship, and you're right...I didn't understand any of that...and he probably wouldn't ever tell me. I don't know what I'll do, but at least now I know what I'm up against and why all this happened."

"Take care, and please, be happy."

Casey landed his plane and taxied to parking at the Las Vegas airport. The sun was bright, bouncing off the asphalt, and even his dark-green aviator glasses didn't shield his eyes from the glare. A flag van led him to an empty parking space and then transported him, along with his luggage and equipment, to the main terminal. He filed his fuel and oil order and left instructions for tie-down.

It was lunchtime. He walked up the stairs to the restaurant automatically, but realized he couldn't eat as soon as he saw and smelled food. He walked back down again past the ever-present slot machines and found the car-rental desk. He filled out the forms and was advised of a fifteen-minute wait before the car could be ready.

The telephones startled him. He hadn't been looking for telephones. He'd just been wandering aimlessly, filling time, trying not to think, and suddenly here he was beside the telephones. On impulse he picked up a receiver and punched in her number. He listened to the ringing, breath held, heart racing. No answer. He hung up the phone with a mixture of immense relief and extreme disappointment. Of course she was at work this time of day. Had he subconsciously known that when he'd dialed? Had he purposely chosen a time when he was relatively certain she wouldn't answer?

What would he have said had she answered? Could he have said anything? Or would he have listened to her voice saying hello and then hung up like the coward he felt himself to be? Could he have laid his feelings bare, taking the risk that she might reject him, or worse, accept him with "conditions"?

Wouldn't forgetting her be the best thing he could do for himself? God, what a stupid thought. He could no sooner forget her than he could forget to breathe. She would be in his mind and in his heart forever.

"Your car's ready now, sir," a pleasant voice said from behind him.

He turned to accept the keys from an attractive young woman. Very young, in fact. Under the makeup he judged her to be twenty or less.

Her eyes grew wide. "Aren't you Casey Cavanaugh?" she asked. "*The* Casey Cavanaugh."

He nodded wearily.

"Oh, wow, I can't believe this! I'm really a fan of yours. I go to all the rodeos that are close enough, and of course I watch you on television. Say, you were super on the *Tonight Show*."

Casey started toward his pile of belongings, and the girl followed him, talking as they went.

"Your autograph! I need to get you to sign something so I can show my friends."

She produced a pen and took off her hat.

"Here, sign the band for me," she giggled. "Then I'll be able to wear your name."

Without comment he took the hat and the pen and scrawled his name on the leather band.

"The match starts tomorrow afternoon, doesn't it? That means you have tonight free, and well, I don't have to work tonight..."

Casey ignored the obvious invitation. She wasn't to be put off so easily, though.

"We could get together," she said pointedly. "I've got all night free."

"Another time, maybe," Casey told her as he swung his gear bag onto his shoulder and hefted his suitcase and saddle. He made an effort at smiling as he said goodbye, but he could tell by the disappointment in her face that he hadn't done a very good job.

He pulled away from the small terminal and out onto a freeway heading toward town and the King Midas Hotel. He thought about the horse he'd drawn for tomorrow. One of the best. A challenge at anytime. Why had he come? He couldn't ride a child's pony in his present frame of mind.

His thoughts drifted back to the phone call he'd tried to make. What in the hell would he have said if she'd answered? He'd never been good at putting his emotions into words, and a phone conversation was the worst possible means, anyway. Thank God she hadn't been home.

All the way to work Paige's mind reeled. She recalled what she'd said to Casey and she realized now how it had sounded to him. The question in her mind now, was, how did she feel? Could she accept his lifestyle? She had never actually thought about it until now. And Casey was right; it was a very real, very pressing consideration.

Three months ago she could have answered without hesitation. Three months ago she could have said without a doubt that no, she couldn't live with a man who traveled so much and took so many risks. Three months ago she wouldn't have had to agonize over the question.

But, then, three months ago she had been a different person. That Paige Bannister was no longer in existence. Three months ago she hadn't even been alive.

Her life did not consist of black and white any longer. The simplicity of clear-cut answers were no longer a luxury she possessed. She no longer knew the answers.

Why shouldn't she ask him to quit? Why shouldn't that be a condition of loving her? Wouldn't that prove he really did love her? Living with a rodeo cowboy would be hard. There would be lonely times and frustrating times and worrying times. There would be times when their schedules wouldn't begin to mesh. There would be times when the thought of him getting hurt would eat away at her. If he would quit and erase all those problems wouldn't life be simpler and happier for both of them?

When Paige walked into her office her phone was ringing. A tiny flame of hope momentarily flared in her mind, but when she answered it wasn't him. Of course it wasn't him.

It was her sister Karen, calling to say she was going to be in San Francisco for the day and wondering if Paige could have lunch. Time and place were arranged, and Paige went back to the miserable task of trying to concentrate on her work.

"You look terrible, Paige," Karen said as they were seated at a table near the back.

"Thanks," Paige said sarcastically. "I'm glad to see you, too."

"Come on. I only meant concern. Haven't you been well?"

"No, I guess I haven't," Paige answered. "Now tell me what you're doing in town and why you aren't in class."

Karen hesitated a moment as though gathering courage. "I've quit school and I'm interviewing for jobs here in Frisco," she said.

"What's wrong with you!" Paige exploded. "Haven't we been through this before. Don't you know how important your education is? What kind of jobs are you qualified for? Are you going to throw away your future just because you're bored?"

"I knew it," Karen said, and started to rise. She threw her napkin down on the table. "I knew you wouldn't listen. You think you know all the answers."

"Wait," Paige said contritely. "Please don't go. I'm sorry. I want to listen."

Her sister eyed her suspiciously, but sank back down into her seat.

"Does Lindy want to quit, too?" Paige asked.

"'No, little sis is still hooked on college," Karen said. "It's just me, as usual."

"Well, go on," Paige said, sighing. "Tell me."

"I'm tired of school," Karen began cautiously. "I'm tired of being sheltered and taken care of, and I'm tired of not making any of my own decisions. I want to get out in the world and be my own person for a while.

"Ever since I was little you've run my life for me. You've made everything so easy for me—too easy. You've taken all the risk out. Sometimes I want to drive too fast or do something reckless just to prove I have some control. I...oh, it's so hard to explain.... I'm almost twenty years old, and I want to try being a grown-up. I want to depend on myself for a change. I want to take a few risks."

Paige was silent for a moment. A hundred thoughts circled in her mind. A thousand regrets arrived to haunt her. She had to swallow hard before she could speak.

"I always thought I was doing the right things for you and Lindy," she began. "I always believed..."

Karen's face softened. "I know," she said. "It's taken me a long time to get past the resentment, but I think I can understand now. That's why I came to talk to you today. That's why I didn't just do everything without telling you. I don't want to hurt you. I know everything you did for me and to me was out of love. But now, if we're ever going to be close, if we're ever going to have an adult relationship, you have to let go of me. You have to let me make my own decisions and control my own life. You have to let me take whatever risks there are."

Tears burned in Paige's eyes. That was the answer to everything. The only way to hold on to people you loved was to let them go, to let them do what they had to do, regardless of the dangers. The only way to hold on to Casey, to keep the love alive, was to accept him and his life just the way they were.

Paige wheeled her car across several lanes of traffic and into the airport turnoff on Bayshore Freeway. Calmly she joined the line of vehicles entering San Francisco International Airport. Her suitcase and hang-up bag were in the back seat. She was going to Las Vegas.

She didn't want to think about that fact just now. If she thought about it too much, if she truly considered the possibilities and the risks, then she knew she could never board the plane. And she was determined to get on that plane. Nothing else was clear in her mind except getting aboard that aircraft. She would be in Vegas by four o'clock. Beyond that— No, she wouldn't think about anything else. Nothing but getting on the plane.

She deposited her bags at curb-side check-in and drove her car to the long-term parking. One thing at a time. Slowly, carefully, handle one thing at a time. She stood in line for her boarding pass and then stood in line again when boarding was announced. She concentrated on the back of whatever person stood in front of her. No thinking. Absolutely no thinking.

As soon as she was seated on the plane she realized that she was now without an objective. Her goal of being on the aircraft when it took off was now achieved. What next? What could she concentrate on to keep her mind occupied?

*Go to the King Midas.*

That sounded harmless enough. *Get a taxi and go to the King Midas Hotel.* Nothing scary in that. She could definitely handle that assignment.

## Chapter Twelve

The King Midas Hotel was enormous. Paige registered at the outrageous curved-brass extravaganza that passed for a desk and had her luggage sent up to her room. She wandered through the casino-lobby and past the individual restaurants and bars that opened off the main floor. She went up the wide curving stairs and looked at the floor-show area and the high-stakes games.

She had never imagined the place would be so big. The chances of just running into Casey in a place this large seemed slim, indeed. The thought was a relief. She had no notion of how to conduct a meeting with him. She wasn't accustomed to baring her feelings.

How could she even begin? Did one simply walk up and say, "Hello, Casey. I am so in love with you that I can't eat or sleep or think about my work, and I would like to find out if there is any chance at all that we could be good together?''

She walked back to the main desk and found out that Casey Cavanaugh was indeed registered. He was occupying a room on the fourth floor with another cowboy. That let going to his room out. She certainly wasn't going to make a spectacle of herself in front of more than one person at a time.

She turned and started slowly through the crowd toward the elevators. That morning's phone conversation came back to her in bits and pieces. Had Judy been right? Was Casey really miserable without her?

She rounded a bank of nickle slot machines and suddenly there he was, directly in front of her, moving across her line of sight toward the elevator. She stopped, breath caught in her throat, heart pounding, and drank in the sight of him. His wide shoulders and narrow hips. The lean, hard grace of his body as he moved. The sharply creased jeans and flawlessly fitted shirt he wore.

Without consciously making the decision, she moved toward him. Like a helpless creature being drawn hypnotically into some kind of lethal trap, she felt pulled to him.

He turned. The planes and angles of his face and the penetrating blue of his eyes were so dreamlike she questioned her own sense of reality. Was this really happening?

"Paige," he said simply, and her heart shattered into a million tiny fragments.

The elevator came and went.

"What are you doing here?" he asked.

"More work on the rodeo project," she lied.

"I can't believe you're here I—I never expected to see you here," he said.

She shrugged and attempted a smile.

"Ever been to Vegas before?" he asked.

"No. I'm looking forward to seeing the town."

"Have you been here long?"

She drew in a deep breath.

"No. I just got in. Haven't even been to my room yet. How about you?"

"Same," he said. "Flew in about an hour ago. I was just going to my room to clean up for dinner."

"Oh," she said, glancing at her watch. "I guess it is about that time, isn't it?"

"Then you haven't eaten, either?"

"No."

There was a momentary silence.

"We could..." she began.

"How about..." he said at the same time.

They both laughed nervously.

"I was just going to say, how about having dinner together? I mean, since you don't know the town or anything?"

"That would be fine," she agreed quickly.

"Meet you here, then, at the elevators, in say, forty-five minutes?"

"Fine," she said.

She closed the door to her room and stood ankle-deep in plush carpeting, surrounded by luxurious appointments, and she knew she should have been awed. Instead all she could think of was that she had never been this close to true insanity in her entire life.

If there were some way to turn back the calendar to a point before she'd met Casey Cavanaugh and make different decisions—decisions that would prevent their ever coming together—would she do it. Did she want to go back to the passionless existence she'd been leading? Why not? At least then she hadn't felt pain, she hadn't known this constant agony.

But she hadn't known the love, either. She hadn't felt the warmth of true sharing with someone. She hadn't known what it was like to need someone. She hadn't known the joy of sexual fulfillment with a man she ached for. God, she hadn't even been alive.

No, she wouldn't change it if she could. In spite of the pain. In spite of the risks involved. But what of the future? The future was something within her grasp. The present was now. Could she break through her own reservations and his, as well? Their future, or lack of it, would be decided this night. What should she do? How should she act to ensure no regrets?

Like a sleepwalker she went through the mechanics of dressing and doing her hair and makeup. Her mind was on one level, while her body functioned separately on another.

She met him at the elevators precisely on time. He was wearing slacks and a sport coat. She'd never seen him in anything but jeans. He looked wonderful, of course. He always looked wonderful.

She walked along the wide, crowded sidewalk beside him, almost touching, but not quite. Huge electric signs twinkled and flashed and changed colors around them. The streets were aglow with lights.

She glanced over at him and caught him looking at her. Their smiles were nervous, self-conscious. She felt as if she'd somehow regressed back to adolescence. Every uncertainty and insecurity she'd ever known rested on her shoulders tonight.

The restaurant was discreetly elegant and very French. The small tables were privately arranged, and most of the lighting was furnished by slender tapers burning in polished-brass wall sconces. She wondered how he had known about it and how he had gotten the reservations.

She watched him go through the ritual of selecting the wine. Every move he made was perfect to her. There could be no man on earth more wonderful than this one. She wanted him to love her. She wanted him to need her as much as she needed him. But she wanted proof of it before she committed herself. She couldn't take the risk again and be hurt again.

The waiter appeared with a pair of burnished-leather dinner menus. Paige accepted hers and opened it, but her mind was not on food. She tried to concentrate on the ornate script of the menu. Each dish was listed in French and then in English. There were no prices. That usually meant the prices were outrageous.

Why had he chosen a place like this? Was he trying to impress her or maybe apologize to her? Or was he just setting her up again for another fall.

Why didn't he say something or do something that would show her how he felt?

The waiter reappeared. At random she selected a chicken dish whose French name she couldn't begin to pronounce. She watched as he ordered. Every word he spoke, every move he made caused the ache inside her to grow sharper.

"How's your work going?" he asked when the waiter left.

"Fine," she said. "I'm up to the point where I could free-lance if I wanted to." She wanted to add that that meant she could work and still travel a great deal. She wanted to add that that made a career and a life with him entirely feasible.

"I thought you were good," he said. "I mean, I liked what you wrote very much."

"Thank you."

"Do you still work with the little girl—what was her name?"

"No," Paige answered evenly. "Her name was Trisha, and she and her mother moved away."

"Oh," he said.

The wine steward presented and poured the wine. She breathed in the perfume of the newly opened wine and the fragrance of the single red rose centered on the table. She watched the flickering flame shadows dance on the walls and across his face.

*Please, Casey,* she pleaded inwardly, *please love me. Please reach out and take my hand or look into my eyes and tell me it was all a mistake. That you were wrong to leave, that you want me and need me.*

"When this rodeo series is over I guess you'll be staying in California," he said.

"Only until I get another story assignment that calls for traveling."

"You're probably anxious to stay home awhile, though."

"No, not really," she said. "I'm not particularly attached to the area I live in. I like traveling, and I

think I could live almost anywhere and be happy.''
Did he hear what she was saying? Did he understand what she was trying to tell him?

The first course was presented, and Casey was silent. She could tell his mind was not on the food, but what was it on? Was he thinking about her?

Was he burning inside for her the way she burned for him? How could she break through and get him to show his feelings?

Casey had no interest in the food. He was too caught up in her presence. Her voice, her manner, her dignified bearing. He knew if he leaned just a fraction closer he would be able to smell her perfume. He would be able to touch her soft shining hair and caress the smooth length of her arm.

His thoughts were in turmoil.

She was so cool and composed. Apparently he'd meant nothing to her. She hadn't even mentioned the letter. She hadn't acted angry or hurt. He obviously hadn't touched her in any way. All of his mental torture was for nothing. He didn't stand a chance with her. He was certain telling her how he felt would only worsen matters.

He watched her eat. Did she have any idea what he was going through? Did she have any sense of the pain he felt?

"Did you draw well here at the match?" she asked.

"Yes," he said, but he wanted to add that it didn't matter. Nothing mattered but the emptiness inside him.

He had to say something. He couldn't leave the subject untouched. He had to at least apologize.

"About the letter," he said in an offhand manner. "I'm sorry about that. I should have stuck around and told you in person."

He watched her carefully. How would she react? Did she have any feelings toward him at all?

Paige cleared her throat softly and reached for a drink of water. She barely trusted herself to speak.

He had finally mentioned something personal between them. It came as a shock. She had begun to think that the evening would consist solely of small talk. That there would never be any kind of an acknowledgment of what had passed between them.

Now suddenly, when she least expected it, he'd mentioned the letter. Mentioned it in such a casual, offhand manner that it was immediately clear to her that the incident held no meaning for him. Certainly he felt some measure of guilt about his handling of the situation, about not having the courage to face her, but that was all. His regrets were not about leaving her, but just the manner in which he'd done it.

Hurt and anger and wounded pride flared inside her. Fine. If that was the way he wanted it, then two could play this game. She'd be damned if she'd let him know the extent of the pain he'd caused her.

"No problem. You were in a hurry." She shrugged. "I understood. It didn't bother me a bit."

"It didn't?" he asked, disappointment creeping into his voice.

"No," she assured him. "Matter of fact, I was having second thoughts myself and I was relieved that you made everything so easy."

"Oh. Good," he said, and gave his attention back to his dinner.

They said little throughout the rest of the meal. There was nothing left to say. All hopes were dead and buried. Paige grieved in a raw, painful silence.

The walk back to the hotel took forever. She breathed in the night desert air and watched the ever-changing lights and wondered where she had gone wrong. Which incorrect turn had been the deciding factor? Exactly when had she lost him? If only she knew and could will herself back in time to do it over again, to do it right this time.

Her pride didn't seem to matter now. What mattered was that she would never walk beside him like this again, that she would never look into his eyes again, that she would never feel the touch of his hands again.

Pride, huh! She would throw away her pride in an instant if she thought it would do any good. She would beg him to change his mind. She would get down on her knees and plead with him to love her—or to at least allow her to love him.

They entered the lobby of the hotel and walked slowly across the figured green carpet.

Silently she prayed for something to happen. A fire. A flood. An earthquake or tornado or hurricane. Anything to keep him from saying goodbye.

Casey held the door for her to enter the hotel lobby, and he was suddenly panic-stricken. This was it. In a matter of minutes she would say goodbye and shut the door to her room, shutting him out of her life forever. He had to think of something. He had to stall. He felt like a man asking for a cigarette on his way to the gallows.

"Ever played the slot machines?" he asked. It was the first thing that popped into his head.

"No," she said. "Have you?"

"Sure. Lots of times. Most of the guys like the table games or the roulette wheels, but I don't care that much for the hard-core stuff. Slots, especially the nickle kind, are a lot of fun without getting into the big money, serious gambling."

"Oh," she said.

He looked around frantically for a cashier's cage. Nickles. He needed some nickles fast.

He bought four large paper cups of nickles. Enough to last hours, he hoped.

"Come on," he said. "You can give her a try."

Relief flooded through Paige. It wasn't over yet. It wasn't goodbye yet. She accepted a cup of nickles from him and wondered how slow she could play without him noticing. How long could she make this last?

They started out on one machine. Carefully he explained all the possibilities for wins. She looked into his eyes and nodded as he described the different lucky combinations, and all she could think of was his nearness.

He fed in a nickle and she gripped the handle, and he placed his hand over hers to pull it down. His touch was devastating. Her knees shook and she couldn't seem to focus on the combinations that appeared when the dials stopped whirling.

They lost a lot. They won some jackpots. She didn't care whether they won or lost. There was no thrill to winning. Winning was important only because it replenished their dwindling supply of nickles. The nickles were her lifeline; they were buying her time. If only she had enough nickles to last a lifetime.

They were down to one cup, when Casey came up with the lucky-machine theory. He said that there was only one lucky machine on each row and that they should work their way through the rows, playing no more than one nickle in any given unit, and search for the lucky machines.

Paige agreed eagerly. Another reprieve. Another way to make the nickles last longer. She went through the rows with him, analyzing the machines, discussing the merits of fruit-versus-cardfaces and any other ridiculous thing that popped into her mind relating to the one-armed bandits. She held her breath each time they pulled a handle. *Please let there be a jackpot,* she pleaded silently. *Please let there be more nickles.*

The end came, of course. She knew it would. The cup was empty. The last nickle was played with no results.

"You're probably tired?" he said, and it was a question.

"Yes," she said.

She was tired of trying to fight something that was so obviously inevitable. She was tired of trying to hold on to something she knew she couldnt possibly have.

They rode silently in the elevator. He insisted on walking her to her door. She unlocked it, then turned back to him to say good-night. The pain was a crushing weight inside her chest.

He wanted to kiss her! It was written on his face clearly. The realization so startled her that she couldn't respond. She was cast in stone, unmoving and unfeeling in her confusion and surprise.

"Night," he said abruptly, and turned.

She watched him walk away down the wide empty hallway. He was almost to the elevator before she found her voice. "Casey," she called to him. "Could you come back here for just a minute."

As soon as she was certain he'd heard, she raced into her room, leaving the door ajar for him. She kicked off her shoes and yanked her dress roughly over her head. When he stepped through the door she was waiting for him in her black silk slip.

He stood there, looking at her, uncertainty in his eyes. She reached behind him and pushed the door shut. He opened his mouth to speak, but she put her fingers to his lips to stop him. Words weren't necessary now. Words would only spoil things. There would be time for words later.

Carefully she took off his hat and set it aside. She ran her fingers through his thick dark hair. He stood silent and unmoving, his eyes fixed on her face. She traced the planes and angles of his face with her fingertips. Slowly she unbuttoned his shirt, pulling it free at the same time. She slipped her hands inside, running them across his chest down to the lean hardness of his belly. She undid his big gold buckle and pulled his belt free.

Still he hadn't moved. His hands hung loosely by his sides. His eyes burned with questions.

She kissed him lightly on his ear, his neck and down across his chest. A trail of kisses. She drank in the smell of him, the feel of him, the taste of him.

She reached down, took hold of his hand and guided it to her breast. She put her other hand on the back of his neck and pulled him down and toward her. She kissed his lips softly at first and then harder.

He moaned. A sound of such incredible pain and anguish that it momentarily frightened her. But there was little time to think. Suddenly his arms were around her, pulling her tighter against him, and his lips were responding hungrily to hers.

There was no tomorrow. There was no reality beyond this.

When it was over she lay beside him in the tangled sheets of the bed, her head resting on his chest, one of her legs flung across his. She would never regret her actions. She would have traded anything, given anything, promised anything for those moments of passion with him.

Any minute now he would leave, but she refused to think about that until it happened. She refused to think about anything but the broad substance of his chest beneath her cheek and the sound of his heart and the rhythm of his breathing.

"Why?" he said, and his words cut sharply into the stillness.

"I just..." She fumbled for words. What should she say? What shouldn't she say? "I just wanted to be with you, to make love to you, one more time."

"Why?" he said again. Was that pain in his voice?

"Because," she said no louder than a whisper.

"It doesn't make sense," he said. "Why would you want this when you don't care about me at all?"

Her mind spun. What on earth was he talking about? Not care about him! A deaf, dumb and blind person could probably tell how much she cared about him.

"What do you mean?" she asked.

"I can't understand you," he said with a sigh. "The way you made love just then—I could have thought that I meant something to you."

She almost laughed. What an understatement! What did he want? Was he fishing for a declaration of love to add to his list of conquests?

"You could say that," she said.

"Say what—that I mean something to you?"

She didn't answer.

He sat up, gripping her shoulders and pulling her up to face him.

"Don't play with me, Paige. Tell me if I mean something to you. Tell me if I have any chance with you at all."

She looked into his eyes and saw that he was deadly serious, that he was absolutely sincere.

She swallowed hard. "Yes," she said in a ragged whisper.

"Yes, what?" he demanded.

"Yes...you mean something to me...you mean a lot to me...you...I love you, Casey. I love you."

"Oh, God," he said, pulling her close to him and burying his face in her hair. "You don't know how much I've wanted to hear those words. I didn't think—God, it doesn't even matter what I thought.

I—I love you more than I ever thought possible. I want you more than anything else in the world. I'll give up rodeo for you. I'll be anything you want me to be. I'll—''

"No!" she cried. "I don't want you to give up anything for me. I love you just the way you are. I can live with whoever you want to be. I love every part of you. Even the part that wants to risk it all riding in rodeos. You could never change what you are, and I don't want you to even try."

"But I thought . . ." he began.

"Hush," she said. "We've got the rest of our lives to work it out. The important thing is that we love each other and we can work it out. We can work anything out as long as we're honest and open with each other, and as long as we love each other enough to take the risks."

When Paige finally awoke it was well into afternoon. She stretched, enjoying the delicious sense of satisfaction and peace she felt. The bed was empty beside her. The bathroom door was half open and the light was on.

"Casey?" she called.

There was no answer. She got up with a mounting sense of dread and walked to the bathroom. It was empty. A heavy weight settled in her stomach. She looked around the room. His hat was gone. His boots were gone. His wallet was gone from the dresser.

She almost laughed. It was like a scene in a movie, rewound and replayed. She felt dead inside, like the hollow shell left by some decayed sea creature. She sank onto the bed and numbly stared at the blank wall.

A key grated loudly in the lock. She jumped up and grabbed her robe, expecting the maid to walk in.

The door swung open, and there was Casey looking cheerful and rested and unconcerned.

"You're up," he said, and then stopped at the sight of her.

"Is there something wrong? Was I gone too long?"

She stood there staring at him, absorbing the fact of his presence.

He took several steps toward her and produced a small blue velvet case.

"I woke up and started thinking about everything this morning," he began. "And I...well—" He paused and cleared his throat. He held the case out toward her. "I didn't know exactly what you liked." He offered the case hesitantly. "But we can exchange it."

She couldn't seem to move.

He flipped open the case, took hold of her limp hand and forced her to take hold of it. Slowly she tore her eyes from his face, lifted the case and looked. Inside, against the dark velvet, rested the most stunning, marquise-cut, diamond solitaire she had ever seen.

"I don't know what to say," she said, shaking her head in disbelief.

"Just say yes."

"Yes," she whispered, tears starting down her cheeks.

She looked away from the ring, into the warmth of his eyes.

"Yes, yes, yes!" She laughed as she stepped into his arms.

# READERS' COMMENTS ON SILHOUETTE SPECIAL EDITIONS:

"I just finished reading the first six Silhouette Special Edition Books and I had to take the opportunity to write you and tell you how much I enjoyed them. I enjoyed all the authors in this series. Best wishes on your Silhouette Special Editions line and many thanks."

—B.H.*, Jackson, OH

"The Special Editions are really special and I enjoyed them very much! I am looking forward to next month's books."

—R.M.W.*, Melbourne, FL

"I've just finished reading four of your first six Special Editions and I enjoyed them very much. I like the more sensual detail and longer stories. I will look forward each month to your new Special Editions."

—L.S.*, Visalia, CA

"Silhouette Special Editions are — 1.) Superb! 2.) Great! 3.) Delicious! 4.) Fantastic! . . . Did I leave anything out? These are books that an adult woman can read . . . I love them!"

—H.C.*, Monterey Park, CA

*names available on request

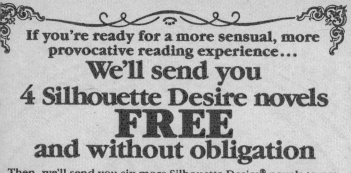

# *Silhouette Special Edition*

## AMERICAN TRIBUTE

### Where a man's dreams count for more than his parentage...

*Look for these upcoming titles under the Special Edition American Tribute banner.*

---

**LOVE'S HAUNTING REFRAIN**
**Ada Steward #289—February 1986**
For thirty years a deep dark secret kept them apart—King Stockton made his millions while his wife, Amelia, held everything together. Now could they tell their secret, could they admit their love?

---

**THIS LONG WINTER PAST**
**Jeanne Stephens #295—March 1986**
Detective Cody Wakefield checked out Assistant District Attorney Liann McDowell, but only in his leisure time. For it was the danger of Cody's job that caused Liann to shy away.

AM-TRIB-1

# Silhouette Special Edition

## AMERICAN TRIBUTE

## AMERICAN TRIBUTE

### RIGHT BEHIND THE RAIN
**Elaine Camp #301–April 1986**
The difficulty of coping with her brother's
death brought reporter Raleigh Torrence
to the office of Evan Younger, a police
psychologist. He helped her to deal with
her feelings and emotions, including love.

### CHEROKEE FIRE
**Gena Dalton #307–May 1986**
It was Sabrina Dante's silver spoon that
Cherokee cowboy Jarod Redfeather couldn't
trust. The two lovers came from opposite
worlds, but Jarod's Indian heritage taught
them to overcome their differences.

### NOBODY'S FOOL
**Renee Roszel #313–June 1986**
Everyone bet that Martin Dante and Cara
Torrence would get together. But Martin
wasn't putting any money down, and Cara
was out to prove that she was nobody's fool.

### MISTY MORNINGS, MAGIC NIGHTS
**Ada Steward #319–July 1986**
The last thing Carole Stockton wanted was to
fall in love with another politician, especially
Donnelly Wakefield. But under a blanket of
secrecy, far from the campaign spotlights,
their love became a powerful force.

# Silhouette Special Edition

## COMING NEXT MONTH

**STATE SECRETS—Linda Lael Miller**
When David joined Holly Llewellyn's cooking class, they found
themselves instantly attracted to each other, but neither of them
could chance falling in love since both had something to hide.

**DATELINE: WASHINGTON—Patti Beckman**
Investigative reporters Janelle Evans and Bart Tagert had different
methods for finding facts, so when they were assigned to the same
story the clashes were inevitable...but the passion was unexpected.

**ASHES OF THE PAST—Monica Barrie**
Although four years had passed since Blair had been widowed,
she was reluctant to become involved, until she met author
Sean Mathias and a mysterious passion drew her to him.

**STRING OF PEARLS—Natalie Bishop**
Devon had once believed the worst of Brittany, now the past was
repeating itself. Brought together again by the pursuit of a smuggler,
could they find the love they had lost?

**LOVE'S PERFECT ISLAND—Rebecca Swan**
Alex Gilbert and Ian McLeod were on opposing sides of a wildlife
issue, until the beauty of the Aleutian Islands lured them away from
their debate and into each other's arms.

**DEVIL'S GAMBIT—Lisa Jackson**
When Zane appeared at Rhodes Breeding Farm insisting that
Tiffany's champion stallion was alive, she had to discover if this
alluring man was trying to help her, or was seeking revenge.

---

## AVAILABLE NOW:

| | |
|---|---|
| **SUMMER DESSERTS** Nora Roberts | **A CLASS ACT** Kathleen Eagle |
| **HIGH RISK** Caitlin Cross | **A TIME AND A SEASON** Curtiss Ann Matlock |
| **THIS BUSINESS OF LOVE** Alida Walsh | **KISSES DON'T COUNT** Linda Shaw |